More Critical Praise for Bernice L. McFadden

for *The Book of Harlan*

• Winner of the NAACP Image Award for Outstanding Literary Work (Fiction)
• Winner of an American Book Award
• A *Washington Post* Notable Book of 2016
• Finalist for a Hurston/Wright Legacy Award

"Simply miraculous . . . As her saga becomes ever more spellbinding, so does the reader's astonishment at the magic she creates. This is a story about the triumph of the human spirit over bigotry, intolerance, and cruelty, and at the center of *The Book of Harlan* is the restorative force that is music." —*Washington Post*

"McFadden packs a powerful punch with tight prose and short chapters that bear witness to key events in early-twentieth-century history . . . Playing with themes of divine justice and the suffering of the righteous, McFadden presents a remarkably crisp portrait of one average man's extraordinary bravery in the face of pure evil."
—*Booklist*, starred review

"Through this character portrait of Harlan, McFadden has constructed a vivid, compelling narrative that makes historical fiction an accessible, literary window into the African American past and some of the contemporary dilemmas of the present."
—*Publishers Weekly*

for *Gathering of Waters*

• A *New York Times* Notable Book of 2012
• Finalist for a Hurston/Wright Legacy Award
• Finalist for a Phillis Wheatley Fiction Book Award

"McFadden works a kind of miracle—not only do [her characters] retain their appealing humanity; their story eclipses the bonds of history to offer continuous surprises . . . Beautiful

and evocative ... *Gathering of Waters* isn't long, but it brings three generations urgently to life ... The real power of the narrative lies ... in the richness and complexity of the characters ... While they inhabit these pages they live, and they do so gloriously and messily and magically, so that we are at last sorry to see them go, and we sit with those small moments we had with them and worry over them, enchanted, until they become something like our own memories, dimmed by time, but alive with the ghosts of the past, and burning with spirits."
—Jesmyn Ward, *New York Times Book Review* (Editors' Choice)

"Read it aloud. Hire a chorus to chant it to you and anyone else interested in hearing about civil rights and uncivil desires, about the dark heat of hate, about the force of forgiveness."
—Alan Cheuse, *All Things Considered*, NPR

"As strange as this may sound, Bernice L. McFadden has created a magical, fantastic novel centered around the notorious tragedy of Emmett Till's murder. This is a startling, beautifully written piece of work."   —Dennis Lehane, author of *Mystic River*

for *Glorious*

• Finalist for the NAACP Image Award for Fiction
• Winner of the BCALA Literary Award for Fiction

"McFadden's lively and loving rendering of New York hews closely to the jazz-inflected city of myth ... McFadden has a wonderful ear for dialogue, and her entertaining prose equally accommodates humor and pathos."
—*New York Times Book Review*

"[McFadden] brings Harlem to astounding life ... Easter's hope for love to overthrow hate ... cogently stands for America's potential, and McFadden's novel is a triumphant portrayal of the ongoing quest."   —*Publishers Weekly*

Raya

BERNICE L. McFADDEN is the author of nine critically acclaimed novels including *Sugar*, *Loving Donovan*, *Nowhere Is a Place*, *The Warmest December*, *Gathering of Waters* (a *New York Times* Editors' Choice and one of the 100 Notable Books of 2012), *Glorious*, and *The Book of Harlan* (winner of a 2017 American Book Award and the NAACP Image Award for Outstanding Literary Work, Fiction). She is a four-time Hurston/Wright Legacy Award finalist, as well as the recipient of three awards from the BCALA.

Also by Bernice L. McFadden

PRAISE SONG

for the

BUTTERFLIES

BY BERNICE L. MCFADDEN

Published by Akashic Books
©2018 by Bernice L. McFadden

Hardcover ISBN: 978-1-61775-575-0
Paperback ISBN: 978-1-61775-626-9
Library of Congress Control Number: 2017956559

This novel appeared in an earlier form as an e-book in 2009 under the title *My Name Is Butterfly*.

Akashic Books
Brooklyn, New York, USA
Ballydehob, Co. Cork, Ireland
Twitter: @AkashicBooks
Facebook: AkashicBooks
E-mail: info@akashicbooks.com
Website: www.akashicbooks.com

For all of those little black girls and little black boys.
For those delicate butterflies, those beautiful innocents.

The word *trokosi* comes from the Ewe words *tro*, meaning deity or fetish, and *kosi*, meaning female slave.

I only ask to be free. The butterflies are free.
—Charles Dickens

A BRIEF HISTORY OF UKEMBY

Shaped like a kinked index finger, confined between Ghana and Togo, Ukemby is a nation about which very little is known before the seventeenth century when the first Portuguese colonist arrived. That said, there are signs of an early British presence, possibly explorers who succumbed to malaria and/or were murdered by the inhabitants who were, in fact, explorers in their own right, having trekked to Ukemby from regions that are now part of Ghana, Benin, Namibia to the south, and as far east as Tanzania.

The Portuguese used Ukemby as a slave-trading post for Europe and the Americas until the Slave Trade Act of 1807, at which point the Portuguese all but abandoned the colony, save for the criminals and undesirables they deserted upon their departure.

The Portuguese withdrawal left the region vulnerable, ultimately making way for the German Empire to invade Ukemby in 1875 and place it under military rule. Many Ukembans were subject to forced labor, building infrastructure and mining diamonds and bauxite.

Following World War I, the Germans relinquished control of the territory, and the US swooped in to fill the void. The Bureau of Ukemby Affairs was soon established and charged with creating schools to educate and assimilate the children to US standards.

Christianity was deemed the new American territory's official religion; the worship of African gods and deities was outlawed and made punishable by flogging.

Children were forbidden to speak Wele, their native language. If discovered doing so, the parents of those children were flogged. If the infraction happened a second time, the tongues of the violators were removed. A third infraction was punishable by death.

Even so, many defiant elders continued to secretly pass on the language, customs, and traditions of their ancestors.

The American trusteeship was dissolved after World War II and Ukemby finally became an independent nation. A new constitution was adopted by referendum, and a democratic election was held in 1949, installing the country's first African prime minister.

In his first official act upon taking office, Prime Minister Mbeke Kjodle abolished all of the assimilation laws and policies that had been put in place by the Americans, freeing the Ukemban people to openly practice their own customs and traditions. Shrine slavery was one of the traditions that ascended from the darkness back into the light.

AFTER

New York City

Summer 2009

On the morning of the day she killed him, the sun sat high and white in a sky washed clean of clouds by an early-morning downpour. A faint rainbow hovered just beyond the abandoned PS 186. The damp air hummed with hip-hop music, car horns, and courting dragonflies.

Wide hips swaying beneath the sweeping, multicolored skirt, flip-flops smacking musically against the wet pavement, Abeo marched down 145th Street with her head held high.

A gold-and-purple straw purse hung in the crook of her elbow, weighed down with four bottles of homemade hair oils, a magazine, a letter from her aunt Thema, a cell phone, and the rusted screwdriver she carried for protection. In all the years Abeo had been working in and around Harlem, she'd only had to brandish the weapon once, and that was when a drunkard threatened to toss his beer can at her because she had not returned his hello.

When Abeo reached Lenox Avenue, she turned the corner and joined two other women waiting at the bus stop. Abeo nodded in greeting. One woman mumbled good morning; the other diverted her eyes to her hands, pretending to examine her perfectly polished fingernails. A bus approached, thick with passengers, and Abeo and the other women climbed aboard, inserted their Metro-Cards into the slot, and pushed their way to the center of the mass.

Lenox Avenue was already bustling with activity—

people traveled the sidewalks, clutching coffee cups from Dunkin' Donuts, hauling plastic bags crammed with groceries, pushing baby carriages.

She exited the bus at 127th Street and continued on foot toward her place of employment—the Queens of Africa Braiding Salon, located on the corner of 125th and Lenox.

She stepped swiftly past the Nigerian, Sudanese, and Guinean hawkers who stood alongside black and sapphire velveteen blankets displaying items for sale: bootlegged CDs, DVDs, East African soaps, oils, incense, and trashy novels.

As she hurried past them, they called out to her: "Something for you today, mama?" Abeo waved her hand and kept walking. Up ahead she could see the hair shop's sign—a gaudy gold-and-green monstrosity illuminated with red lights. Standing beneath the sign was Mohammed, an elderly man the color of black sand, with a beard as white as cotton. His back was bent, but his eyes were as effervescent as a newborn. Mohammed sold roasted peanuts from a silver pushcart, and he and Abeo were passing acquaintances. Abeo knew that he was a widower, had three children and eight grandchildren, and that he had been in these United States for half a century, never once returning to his homeland of Ukemby. Mohammed knew that Abeo was married with two children and that she worked as a braider and had not been back to Ukemby since she'd arrived in New York in the winter of 2003. Those were the things they knew about each other and not much else.

When Abeo spotted him, she raised her hand in greeting, and in that moment she realized with great

horror that she knew something else about Mohammed; she knew the man standing beside him. Her heart
jumped into her throat and her bladder let go, streaming
urine down her legs.

His name was Duma and she'd known him as inti-
mately as a man of the cloth knew his god—or more
appropriately, the way a sinner knows The Evil One.

Abeo watched frozen as Duma tossed a roasted pea-
nut into the air, tilted his head back, and opened his
mouth. The nut bounced off his bottom lip, fell to the
ground, and rolled across the pavement toward Abeo.
When it bumped the rounded rubber toe of her flip-flop,
she uttered a strangled cry and sprung into the air.

Mohammed gave her a curious look. The smile on
his lips faded to a frown when he saw the frightened ex-
pression on her face. His eyes swung to Duma and then
back to Abeo, just as she started her charge. Teeth bared
she barreled toward them with the screwdriver raised
high above her head.

BEFORE

PORT MASI, UKEMBY

1978—1985

1

A beo's first memory was from a Saturday in 1978. She was two years, eight months, and twenty-three days old the morning she awoke in her parents' large mahogany bed. The room was shrouded in the gray haze of early morning. Outside, a car engine roared to life, the rusty hinges of a wrought-iron gate squealed open, and a choir of roosters began to crow.

Abeo rubbed the sleep from her eyes, searched the room for signs of her parents, and in her quest caught sight of her dark face and button nose in the oblong mirror that hung over the chest of drawers.

Abeo yawned before calling out, "Mama!" over and over until her mother, Ismae Kata, appeared in the doorway.

"What is all this noise, little one, heh?" Ismae cooed. Abeo grinned and raised her chubby arms.

Ismae was slight in build, with the fingers of a pianist—long, thin, and elegant. Her cocoa-colored skin was unblemished, and fragrant with gardenia-scented soap. She lifted Abeo from the bed, set her on her hip, and carried her into the dining room where she placed the little girl into a chair directly across the table from her father, Wasik Kata.

Wasik was reading the *Daily Mirror* newspaper. Abeo

could see his shiny, creased forehead floating above the top of the page.

"Good morning, Papa!" she sang.

Wasik lowered the paper to reveal a square chin and a wide, flat nose that barely supported his thick black-framed glasses. He flashed a gap-toothed smile. "Is that little Abeo?"

She nodded her head vigorously. "Yes, Papa, it's me!"

"No, you cannot be Abeo," he teased. "Abeo is a sleepyhead who never rises this early."

"It's me, Papa, it's me!"

Ismae laughed and placed a loving hand on her husband's shoulder. "Hurry now, you don't want to be late."

The Kata family lived in an affluent section of Port Masi known as the Palm Tree Residential Area. It was a neighborhood comprising expensive homes shaded by the fronds of towering palm trees. They lived in a lovely one-level, mahogany-shingled home with sweeping front and back verandas, tiled floors, and louvered windows. The kitchen was spacious and fitted with all manner of modern conveniences, including a refrigerator that dispensed water from the door and made ice cubes in the freezer.

Wasik and Ismae were from Prama, a rural village located in the Zolta region of Ukemby. Wasik left Prama as a young man, traveling to Port Masi to live with an older brother who, recognizing the intelligence and potential of his younger sibling, eventually sent him off to England to receive a formal education. After graduating from university, Wasik returned to Ukemby and found employment as an accountant in the government's treasury department. He and Ismae had played together as children, but had not seen each other since he'd left Prama. The next time he laid eyes on her, he was reading the *Daily Mirror* and there she was in the newspaper, smiling seductively from the passenger seat of a luxury automobile.

He called the paper and they connected him with the talent agency of which Ismae was a client. Three days later, they had dinner. Four months after that, he proposed and she agreed to become his wife.

That was some years ago, and with the arrival of Abeo, Ismae had exchanged her modeling career for that of a primary school teacher. Wasik was concerned that this new domesticated life was too boring and unfulfilling for a woman whose face had graced advertising billboards, fashion magazines, and who was once rumored to be keeping romantic company with an English nobleman.

Whenever he asked, "Do you miss your other life?" Ismae understood this to mean: *Are Abeo and I enough for you?* Ismae's response was always the same—she'd take Wasik's face tenderly in her hands, press a gentle kiss to his lips, and say: "There is nothing to miss. You and Abeo are the life I've always dreamed of having."

This would quell Wasik's insecurities for the moment. Though for the life of their union, Wasik would continue to raise the question.

They were a privileged family. Wasik drove a silver Mercedes and had his eye on a piece of beachfront property in Tako, where he hoped to build a second home where his family could spend their holidays. Eventually, of course, he and Ismae would retire there, enjoying their golden years by the ocean and spoiling the many grandchildren he imagined they'd have.

They were practicing Catholics, having converted when missionaries came to their village and warned them that they would be damned to hell if they refused to accept Jesus Christ as their Lord and Savior.

Wasik's parents had balked at a religion that only recognized one supreme being and ignored the spirits, ancestors, and minor gods who tended to the sun, river, moon, and animal and plant kingdoms—and so would not allow Wasik to discard his traditional religion for a white god with blond hair and blue eyes. Wasik had to wait until he was out from under his parents' influence before he could convert. Ismae's parents, however, bought in hook, line, and crucifix.

2

The summer Ismae's sister came to visit, Abeo was an impressionable five-year-old. Serafine Vinga was six years younger than Ismae and possessed the same cocoa-colored complexion and lush hair. But unlike Ismae, Serafine was curvy—bottom- and top-heavy. She favored clothing that accentuated those attributes: miniskirts, low-cut blouses, tight jeans, and high heels. Serafine drank and smoked and had a wantonness about her that made other women—including Ismae—uncomfortable. Her years of living in America had imparted in Serafine a twang that made her sound like a *buckruh*—a white person.

She loved music—Ghanaian highlife, Ukemban pop, American R&B, and disco. That year, she came to Ukemby with a black case full of cassettes which she played one after the other, raising the volume on Wasik's stereo higher and higher until the sound filled all the rooms of the house and could be heard out on the street. During those times, Serafine would grab Abeo by the hands and the two would dance until their limbs ached.

Abeo was enchanted with her aunt.

"One day, Abeo," Serafine tweaked her nose and announced, "I am going to send for you to come and spend a vacation with me in America."

"Really?"

"Uh-huh, and I'll take you to McDonald's and Burger King—"

"What is that?"

"You don't know?"

Abeo shook her head.

"Well, they're wonderful restaurants that make delicious hamburgers and milkshakes!"

Abeo licked her lips.

Ismae snorted. "That food is garbage. It's American trash and I won't have my child eating it."

Serafine and Ismae looked at each other and something passed between them sharp enough to cut the air. Finally, Serafine returned her gaze to Abeo. "So, tell me, do you have a boyfriend?"

Abeo made a face. "Yuck!"

Serafine laughed. "So you don't like boys?"

Abeo shook her head.

"Don't worry, one day you will. One day you will love them."

Months after Serafine had returned to her life in America, Ismae realized that she was feeling more drained and lethargic than usual. She was severely anemic and the disorder had always played havoc with her menstrual cycle, so she didn't think anything was wrong—or in this case, right—when two months passed and she still had not seen her period. It was the light-headedness and the nausea that washed over her whenever she smelled cooked meat—that and the unmistakable flutter deep down in the pit of her belly—that finally alerted her.

Ismae had had so many false alarms in the past that

she dared not say anything to Wasik before she was 100 percent sure. When Dr. Jozy confirmed that she was indeed with child, she sat blinking and mute for ten whole minutes.

That evening, when she shared the news with Wasik, his face lit up like a candle.

"Are you sure?"

Nodding, Ismae wrapped her arms protectively around her midsection.

Wasik pulled her into him, hugging her tightly. "I can't believe it." His words were choked with happiness. "After so many years, finally, God has answered our prayers."

"I always knew that He had not forsaken us," Ismae said.

"All in His time," Wasik whispered into her neck.

Agwe was born in the spring—a round brown boy with pink gums and sparkling eyes. Wasik finally had a son; he could not have been more proud. His family was complete.

Abeo spent most of her free time staring at Agwe. He was the most wondrous thing she had ever seen. "I love him more than crisps," she chanted joyfully. That said a lot, because crisps were Abeo's absolute favorite treat.

3

It was dinnertime when the call came from a cousin who'd walked four miles from Prama to a pay phone. When Wasik answered, an angry evening wind whipped the palm trees surrounding the house, creating static on the line. "Hello?"

"This is Djiimy."

"Djiimy?" Wasik moved the phone to his other ear. "Djiimy?" he echoed shakily, already sensing the bad news.

"Your papa has passed away," Djiimy stated thinly.

Outside, the wind whipped again and lightning flashed across the sky.

"Hello? Djiimy? Hello?" Wasik cried into the receiver.

The line crackled and went dead.

The next day he packed his family into the car and drove to Prama. The trip took four hours and when they arrived, the Mercedes was covered in red dust. As they entered the village, a group of children—the boys indistinguishable from the girls—began running alongside the car, tapping the windows and waving.

When they reached the hut where Wasik had been born and raised, they found his mother seated outside on a stool, picking through a gourd filled with dried peas.

Wasik leaped from the car and bounded over to her, wailing, "Mama, oh Mama!"

Abeo's visits to Prama had always been filled with delight and discovery: the wonder of watching a goat give birth, fetching freshly laid eggs from the chicken coop, drinking warm milk straight from the udder of a cow. But she sensed that this visit would be different. The frenzied excitement that normally accompanied the preparation and four-hour journey was marred by her father's dark melancholy. At the petrol station on their way out of town, Wasik, who was sitting behind the wheel waiting for the attendant to finish filling the tank, suddenly melted into uncontrollable sobs. This frightened Abeo because she had never seen her father—or *any* man—cry.

Abeo now climbed from the car clutching her Walkman protectively to her chest. The circle of children closed in, pointing fingers and probing.

"What is that?"

"Can I have it, sister?"

"What is that? Did you bring one for me?"

"What is that, sister?"

Abeo broke free, fled to her grandmother, threw her arms around her neck, and inhaled a sour mixture of sweat and grilled meat.

The old woman squeezed Abeo, kissed her cheeks, patted her backside, told her that she was too thin, offered her a mango, eyed the silver-and-black contraption the girl held in her hands, and shook her head in dismay.

Grandmother's home was a three-room, thatched-roof mud hut. The front room held two metal chairs with tattered green cushions and one short square table made of wood. A yellowed calendar depicting the deceased prime minister Mbeke Kjodle hung on the wall near the door. The back rooms were furnished with twin-size beds, grass sleeping mats, and nothing else. The cooking area was located behind the house and consisted of three piles of stones beneath an awning made of grass. There was no indoor plumbing, just a standpipe in the middle of the compound where the women lined up daily to fill their buckets with water for cooking, drinking, and bathing. Not too far from the standpipe was the communal toilet, which was little more than a concrete box with a hole in the ground.

In the days leading up to their father's burial, Wasik and his brothers were fitted for the special funeral garments—red-and-gold dashikis. While the tailor labored away, the carpenter constructed a coffin from a forty-year-old walnut tree. An artisan was hired from the neighboring village to carve the coffin with details that reflected the senior Kata's life as a farmer, husband, and father.

The cost was high, a staggering three thousand cendi. Wasik's brothers grumbled at the price, but Wasik said he didn't care if it was thirty thousand cendi; his father deserved the best.

The nights in Prama were long and black. Strange sounds echoed in the darkness and turned sinister in Abeo's imagination. Mating cats became feuding lions; the patter of feet—a charging elephant. She pressed her trembling body against the bulk of her grandmother until the music of the old woman's heart lullabied her to sleep.

On the day of the funeral, large black-and-red tents

were erected at the graveyard. Vendors sold handkerchiefs and beer to the mourners. The village elders beat their breasts and wailed. Sitting to the right of the coffin were long tables draped in red cloth piled high with offerings of money, food, and liquor. The funeral attendants distributed laminated programs that pictured the deceased Kata. Abeo stared down at the photograph of her grandfather; his black eyes watched her from beneath his furrowed brow. She had been fond of him, but did not feel sadness because her young mind could not comprehend the fact that death was final. Even as he lay stiff and cold in the open casket, she watched him expectantly, anticipating the moment when he would sit up and ask her to fetch his smoking pipe.

The interment of the body marked the end of the mourning period and the beginning of the celebration.

Slowly, people pushed their sadness aside, gathered around the tables, and piled their plates high with red-black, *fungee*, fried fish, pepper stew, bread, and fresh fruit. Libations were spilled in honor of the deceased, and then consumed.

Soon, the mourners were laughing and dancing to the syncopated rhythms of bola drums and kazoos.

Abeo, fairly satisfied with Ismae's explanation as to why her grandfather had been placed in a box, joined her cousins in a game of hide-and-seek, while the adults drowned themselves in plum wine and schnapps.

The merriment went on until the darkness seeped from the sky and a new day was upon them.

In the tiny bed Abeo's parents shared, Wasik turned to his wife and mumbled something.

Ismae giggled. "What did you say?"

Wasik's eyes rolled drunkenly in his head. He cleared his throat and repeated, "I will bring Mama to stay with us for a little while." The words dripped like sap from his mouth.

Ismae stroked his forehead. "Of course, Wasik. Whatever you think is best. Now sleep, sweet husband, sleep."

4

To Grandmother, Port Masi smelled of smoke, steel, and shit. She thought her son's house was too grand and reminded Wasik that he was not a king or a chief, so the number of rooms was unnecessary, especially for a family with just two children. She had raised eight children in her modest hut.

"And why is the food cooked inside the house?" she barked, turning her nose up in revulsion.

Wasik bought a television and placed it on the small wooden chest in her bedroom. Grandmother eyed it suspiciously. The last time she'd watched television had been a decade earlier when she'd visited her daughter-in-law's family. Wasik proudly handed her the remote control to the TV. She looked at the little white object and then back at Wasik. "What am I to do with this?"

The next day Wasik bought her a radio.

Grandmother spent her days roaming the house, examining the souvenirs that friends had purchased abroad and given as gifts to the Katas: a white man on a surfboard, a pointed tower, a grand clock. The words stamped on the souvenirs—*Hawaii*, *Paris*, *London*—meant nothing to Grandmother because her language was Wele and her English was limited to *hello* and *goodbye*.

In Abeo's room, Grandmother picked up and then

tossed down the stuffed animals that were neatly arranged across her bed. She reached for the snow globe on the nightstand, shook it, and watched the bits of white plastic swirl and settle on a tiny castle. She pressed her fists into her hips and stared at the poster of a galloping pink horse with a large spiral thorn jutting from the center of its forehead. *Such frivolity*, Grandmother thought to herself, sucking her teeth in disgust.

Another annoyance for Grandmother was the house girl Ismae had hired to cook and clean for the family. Bembe was a fifteen-year-old unwed mother who had gone and gotten herself pregnant at the same time her own mother had conceived. Both mother and daughter were in their second trimesters by the time Bembe confessed her transgressions.

They gave birth within a week of one another. Bembe a cedar-colored boy and her mother twin girls. Within a week their family bloomed from five to eight. Bembe's parents didn't make enough money to clothe and feed them all so Bembe had to drop out of school and find work.

Sweet and quiet, Bembe wasn't the best cook or cleaner, but she was company to Abeo and helpful with Agwe.

For the first few weeks that Grandmother was there, she would not speak to Bembe. Instead, she silently watched, stalking her like a snake in tall grass. Grandmother's silence and cold, hard gaze raised the fine hairs on the back of Bembe's neck.

"I don't trust her," Grandmother muttered. "She has the fingers of a thief. She cleans like a blind woman . . . You call that *jollof*? I call it pig slop!"

Ismae and Wasik smiled and listened respectfully to the old woman's grievances, but did nothing to change the situation, and so one day Grandmother changed it for them.

Wasik was at work, Abeo was at school, and Ismae had taken the baby to visit a friend. When Grandmother heard Bembe set a large metal pot onto the stove, she emerged from her room like a crow and flew into the kitchen squawking demands: "Show me how to work this stove. Fill this pot with water! Chop this . . . cut that . . ."

A flustered Bembe complied without question.

When Ismae returned home, Grandmother was standing over the stove stirring a pot of stew and Bembe was cowering in the corner.

"Mama, what are you doing? We have Bembe to do that," Ismae said.

"I told you, her food tastes like pig slop," Grandmother responded without looking up from her task. "Anyway, what am I to do, sit in that room all day listening to the radio and staring at the picture box?"

"Of course we don't expect that. But you're here to rest, not work. Take a walk; the streets are safe, very safe. No harm will come to you. There are eyes everywhere. Our neighbors know who you are."

Grandmother dropped a pinch of salt into the stew and swirled the wooden spoon around a few times before bringing it to her lips for a taste. Satisfied, she nodded her head and then looked at Ismae. "You should have left me in Prama. This place is hell."

Later, in the privacy of their bedroom, Ismae gently massaged her husband's tense back.

"It'll get better," she offered softly. "Everything is new to her. It's just going to take more time than we thought." She found a knot near his spine and began to work it loose.

Wasik leaned into her kneading fingers. He grunted in agreement, but in truth, his mother was the very least of his worries. What was paramount in his mind was the allegation that had come down from the ministry of finance accusing Wasik's superior—Ota Weli—of diverting government money into a personal account. As a result, Ota had been suspended from work while the powers that be investigated the theft.

Wasik had been summoned to the minister's office and questioned about the matter.

I had no idea, Wasik explained to the minister, wringing his hands. He did not understand why he was so nervous, because he was in no way involved and knew nothing of the theft. But still, perspiration gathered in beads across his forehead, and even as he declared his innocence, his tongue turned to sandpaper.

Really? None at all? the minister had pressed in a gruff voice. *You are his right-hand man and you didn't notice that these funds were missing from the account?*

No sir, I did not. Those particular books were not put in my charge.

The minister eyed him warily. *The truth will be revealed*, he warned, and then dismissed Wasik from the room.

"Did you hear me, Wasik?" Ismae whispered, her lips close to his ear. Her warm breath fanned across his cheek. Wasik turned and peered into her eyes.

"I'm sorry, Ismae," he murmured, bringing her hand to his lips. "I was thinking about something. What did you say?" He kissed her fingers.

Ismae grinned. "I said to stop worrying yourself about your mother, everything is going to be just fine."

"Of course it will," Wasik said, pushing Ismae down onto the bed.

5

One day, a few weeks after Grandmother arrived, Ismae came wobbling into the house supported by her husband and a pair of crutches.

Grandmother spat, "That is what happens when you wear those awful high-heeled shoes."

Ismae ignored the comment. "It was the silliest thing," she stammered. "I go up and down those steps at least once a week. How I missed the last step, I don't know. Thank God I wasn't carrying Agwe!"

Wasik helped Ismae onto the couch and placed a pillow beneath her injured ankle.

Grandmother studied the cast. "How long will you have that thing on your leg?" she asked, running her finger across the hardened plaster.

"The doctor said six weeks."

"Six weeks?" Grandmother responded with a huff.

"Yes."

Grandmother shrugged, turned, and walked into the kitchen grumbling about high-heeled shoes and tight skirts.

Ismae thought how helpful it would be to have Bembe there during her time of need. But the poor girl had crumbled under Grandmother's tyrannical reign, and had found employment elsewhere.

One afternoon during the second week of Ismae's convalescence, she was sitting on the couch flipping through a magazine when Wasik arrived home early from work.

Ismae gazed at her husband's wan and worried face. "What is it? What has happened, Wasik?"

He dropped his briefcase on the floor, went to the glass tray of liquor, and reached for the bottle of schnapps. "They have suspended me," he squeaked.

Ismae tossed the magazine aside. "Did you say *suspended*?"

Wasik took a gulp of the schnapps, swallowed, and nodded.

"But why?"

"They think I have something to do with the money that was stolen."

Ismae already knew about the theft, because news of it had reached the papers. Even as the reports gained momentum, however, Wasik had kept the fact that he was being investigated a secret from her. But now the truth was out in the open.

"That's ridiculous. You've been working at the treasury department for years, and not a cendi has ever gone unaccounted for."

Wasik drained his glass and poured another. When he'd emptied the glass a second time, he brought it close to his face and peered at the empty bottom as if his life had fallen down into it.

"How long will you be suspended?"

"Until the investigation is complete and they find me innocent."

"And how long will that take?" Panic pealed like bells in Ismae's voice.

The schnapps circulated quickly through Wasik's bloodstream, raising his body temperature, burning away the worry. He poured a third drink. "I don't know," he replied dryly.

"What will we do for money?"

Wasik swirled the liquid round and round in the glass. His head felt as light as a leaf. He sighed. "I will still be receiving some of my salary."

"Some?"

"Half."

"Half? We can't live on half!"

Wasik downed the drink, reached for the bottle a fourth time, but thought better of it when Ismae cried, "Wasik, for goodness sakes!"

"We have our savings," he mumbled, "but I can't imagine this investigation will go on long enough for us to have to dip into it."

Ismae let out a bitter laugh. "Have you forgotten where you live? This is Ukemby. What might take a few weeks in other countries can take months or even years here." She shifted uncomfortably on the couch and then timidly added, "I could go back to work."

Wasik made a face and pointed a long finger at her cast.

"It'll be off soon."

He shook his head. "No, you need to be here with the baby. Don't worry."

In the kitchen, Grandmother tiptoed away from the doorway where she had been eavesdropping, went to the stove, and turned the burner on under the pot of cold stew.

* * *

Days later, Agwe developed a cough, followed by a fever that raised boils the size of quail eggs all over his body. Wasik took him to the pediatrician, who prescribed a salve and antibiotics.

The fever broke the next day, but the boils remained.

Grandmother did not trust doctors or their medicine, so she went to the market and bought herbs, which she then pounded into a paste and put in a pot of boiling water. The concoction produced a stench so strong it could be smelled for blocks.

Ismae appeared at the doorway of the kitchen with her hand pressed over her nose and mouth, speaking through the slats of her fingers: "What is that?"

"Medicine for the child."

"Bush medicine?"

"What else would it be?"

Ismae hobbled over and stared into the pot. "Is he to drink that?"

"No, it is for him to wash in."

Ismae backed away from the bubbling mixture, went to the window, and flung it open.

"I-I," Ismae began respectfully, "I don't think this is a good idea. The medicine the doctor prescribed will start to work very soon, so . . ." Her words dropped away under Grandmother's icy gaze.

"You trust some doctor's medicine over that of your own kind?"

Ismae blinked. "Own kind?" Dr. Lama was black and African just like her. Just like Grandmother. "Well, I think that—"

Grandmother slammed the spoon down onto the stove. "What do you think? Tell me, Ismae."

Grandmother had never before used that hard and brittle tone with Ismae and it rattled her. The blood drained from her face, her lips continued to flap, but no words came from her mouth. Finally, wounded, she retreated to her bedroom, took an aspirin for the throbbing headache the encounter had brought on, and soon fell fast asleep.

Hours later, she was startled awake by Agwe's terrified screams. For a few moments Ismae floundered helplessly in and out of sleep, unable to decipher whether or not she was dreaming. When it became clear that Agwe was in peril, she jumped from the bed and landed on her wounded ankle. The pain shot up her leg and exploded behind her eyes. She fell back on the bed, cradling her foot.

Agwe's wails came again, cresting like waves. Ismae hurriedly reached for her crutches and hobbled out of the bedroom.

"Mama! Mama, what are you doing?" Ismae screamed as she entered the bathroom.

Grandmother had Agwe in the bathtub, one meaty arm wrapped tight around his squirming body. The other hand clutched a sponge dripping with the concoction she'd brewed. She dragged the sponge over the boils on Agwe's shoulders, creating a seeping trail of ruptured flesh.

The baby boy screamed again, his howls bouncing off the tiled walls like Ping-Pong balls.

Ismae lumbered forward, throwing herself at Grandmother, who was shorter than her, but wider and stronger. The old woman barely shuddered when Ismae's body slammed into hers.

She caught hold of Grandmother's wrists and tried to twist the hand holding the sponge away from Agwe, but Ismae's own hand slipped and slid on Grandmother's wet flesh. Grandmother shoved her aside, plunged the sponge into the pot of bush medicine, and prepared to swipe it over Agwe's head.

Ismae righted herself, ignored the fresh wave of pain erupting in her ankle, and lunged at Grandmother a second time, sinking her fingernails into the fleshy underside of her arm. The old woman bellowed in agony and surprise before she toppled off the stool and hit the floor with a thump.

When Wasik arrived home from his hearing at the treasury department, Grandmother was seated on the veranda, solemnly plucking the feathers from the body of a decapitated fowl.

"Mama," Wasik said in a tired voice, "I've asked you a hundred times not to do this on the front veranda. If you must buy and kill live fowl, you can clean it in the backyard."

Grandmother raised her head; her lips were pressed into a thin, angry line.

"What's wrong? What's happened?" Wasik asked half-heartedly. He had come to terms with his mother's incessant discontent. It seemed that nothing could please her. So he no longer tried. He simply accepted his role as a sounding board for her daily complaints. He just needed a glass or two of schnapps to get through it.

"Wait, don't tell me," he said, raising his hand. "Let me get a drink first."

"Your wife hit me," she blurted out before he could take a step.

Wasik was sure he'd heard wrong. He set his brief-case down on the empty chair next to his mother. "Sorry?" he offered as he loosened the knot in his tie.

Grandmother flung her arm out at him, revealing the torn flesh. An astonished Wasik gazed stupidly at the gaping wound.

"Ismae did this?"

"Yes," Grandmother snapped.

Wasik's life was bad enough. The officials at the ministry of finance claimed to have incriminating evidence as well as an eyewitness who could confirm Wasik's involvement in the theft. When he asked to see the proof and the name of the eyewitness, the officials denied both requests. Instead, they'd thrust an affidavit under his nose and demanded he sign it. *We can make this go away for you, Kata. No prosecution and no jail time, just dismissal.*

Wasik quickly understood that they didn't have anything on him, but were looking for a scapegoat to take the fall. Talk was, they'd discovered that the real coconspirator was related to the prime minister and thus virtually untouchable.

Wasik knew if he signed the document he would destroy his career and his reputation. He shoved the paper away, excused himself from the meeting, and went straight to an attorney to whom he paid a 10,000-cendi retainer—a quarter of what was in their savings account. And just when he thought the day, his life, couldn't get any worse, he'd come home to find that his wife had assaulted his mother.

Wasik left Grandmother on the veranda and stormed into the house. Abeo was seated at the dining room table immersed in her homework. Her head bounced up when he entered the room.

"Hi, Papa," she chimed.

Wasik forced a smile. "Hello, my beautiful daughter." He'd greeted Abeo this way every day of her life. But this time the words were strained. If Abeo noticed, she didn't react.

"Did you have a good day, Papa?"

Wasik glanced at the wall that separated the dining room from the master bedroom. "I did."

"I think Mama and Agwe are taking a nap. I haven't seen them since I got home from school."

Wasik's face flushed with relief. He was glad that Abeo hadn't been there for all of the ugliness between Ismae and his mother. He bent over and planted a kiss on the top of Abeo's head. "Yes, Mommy is very tired," he said, before asking, "So, did you learn a lot in school today?"

"Oh yes." Abeo leaned over to retrieve her book bag, but when she was erect again, Wasik was already walking out of the dining room.

The bedroom door was closed and locked. Wasik knocked, and when Ismae did not immediately respond, he knocked louder.

"Ismae, open this door now," he hissed. "Do you want Abeo to see us behaving in such a way?"

The lock clicked open and Wasik charged in. Ismae was seated on the edge of the bed, her hair splayed about her head like a madwoman. Her eyes were red from crying. Agwe was sound asleep, naked save for a diaper.

"What have you done?"

"What have I done? What have I done?" Ismae

screeched. "Look, look at your son's skin. Look at it!"

Wasik gazed down at the gaping purple craters on Agwe's body. Before he could catch the words, they flew out of his mouth: "They look like they're healing. Isn't this what we wanted—"

Ismae hurled one of her crutches at him. It clipped his chin and clattered to the floor.

"I-Ismae!" Wasik cried, backing away from her.

Never once in all the years they'd been married had their disagreements turned physical. In fact, Ismae was as nonviolent as they came. Yet here she was, somehow transformed into a ball of ferocity, committing two acts of violence in one short day.

Wasik didn't know what evil had swooped down on his life, or what devil had taken possession of his wife; what he did know was that he needed this bad luck and bad behavior to come to an end.

He bent over, calmly retrieved the crutch, and set it against the wall. "Ismae," he started gently, "can we talk about this civilly?"

"There's nothing to talk about, Wasik. She did what she did and I did what I did. There's no going back to change any of it. And I'm not sorry, so don't ask me to apologize, because I won't." Fresh tears welled up in Ismae's eyes. "I want her out of this house. Today. This minute. Get in your car and drive her back to Prama."

Wasik's Adam's apple bobbed in his throat. He was caught between two bookends, between two women he loved and cherished. He had no idea what he should do.

That evening, Grandmother ate her dinner in the kitchen. The cold silence in the dining room was more than Abeo could bear. Eager to escape the tension, she scoffed down her food and excused herself from the table.

Sometime during the night, Abeo woke to use the bathroom and heard the hushed voices of her father and grandmother. They were conversing in Twel, a Ukemban patois that Abeo was not fully versed in. She was able to catch a few words, including her name and Serafine's, which was mentioned several times.

Grandmother made a remark about bad luck, followed by a million words Abeo did not understand.

Although she could not grasp what was being debated, Abeo did recognize the urgency in her grandmother's tone, even as Wasik's responses sounded unsure.

6

It was a known but seldom discussed fact that Ismae's grandfather, Nsun Vinga, had brought shame and bad luck onto his family.

When Nsun was fourteen years old, a group of white tourists came to visit his village. They arrived with cameras swinging from their pale necks, bottles of bug spray and rolls of toilet paper tucked into their knapsacks. They brought gifts of crayons, coloring books, pencils, notebooks, and candy for the children. For the adults—secondhand clothing, soap, deodorant, large tubs of Vaseline, and sanitary napkins.

The white people arrived in a dented passenger van that belched brown smoke from its exhaust pipe. It was that van that started the problems for Nsun. The driver had left the keys in the ignition—Nsun spotted this, climbed into the vehicle, turned the key, and the engine sputtered to life. He'd never been in an automobile before and so he sat there pressing the pedals with his feet and laughing at the sound of the motor racing away beneath the hood. After a few moments, he took hold of the gear stick, pulled it toward him, and the vehicle began to roll backward. Nsun yipped in surprise and glee.

Hearing the noise, the driver rushed out from the hut he'd been resting in and hurried toward the moving vehicle. Nsun, unable to stop the van from rolling, leaped out and took off running. The van rolled over a wire fence, down a hill, and into a herd of grazing goats, crushing two female kids.

Nsun was caught and punished with a severe whipping, which left scars on his body that he would take to his grave. His father promised the owner of the goats that he would replace the dead property; but he was a poor man and never had enough money to honor that pledge. To make matters worse, those particular goats were not just animals kept for milk, flesh, and hide; they were pets. In fact, they were the owner's favorite pets. The death of the goats left the owner inconsolable, and three months after the unfortunate incident, the old man succumbed to a broken heart and died. So the wrong was never set right and this, of course, displeased the gods.

Nsun went on to live a long and fairly happy life. Yet his offense was still alive and well and lurked among his descendants like a specter, awaiting retribution. That time, according to Grandmother, had finally arrived.

It seemed to be true.

Wasik had not taken Grandmother back to Prama and this act—or non-act—created a wedge between Wasik and Ismae.

Ismae had moved into the guest room and taken Agwe with her.

The investigation was still dragging on, there seemed to be no end in sight, and the money in his bank account was disappearing as quickly as if he'd set a match to it. Soon they'd be penniless, and then what would they do?

Grandmother caught Wasik firmly by the chin one evening and forced him to look into her lined face.

"Things are getting worse for you. Think about your wife and your son."

Wasik cringed, tried and failed to pull away from her vise grip.

"I know you love her, but she is not *your* daughter, she is not of *our* blood. It is the Vinga's family sin to fix; if she won't do it, then you must."

"But Mama—"

"Take Abeo to a shrine and offer her to the gods. Then and only then will things get better for you."

And with that, she released him and lumbered off to her bedroom.

When Wasik took the solution to Ismae, her hand fluttered to her parted lips to block the laughter chugging up from her throat. Little good it did. When it reached her lips, the laughter plowed through her fingers and exploded into the room.

Wasik watched in silence, the corners of his mouth twitching. True, Ismae's laughter was infectious, but more than that, Wasik realized just how ridiculous his suggestion sounded.

When Ismae finally composed herself, she dabbed the corners of eyes, asking, "You're joking, right?"

Wasik tried to smile, but only one side of his mouth cooperated.

"Yes, of course I'm joking," he chuckled ashamedly.

Ismae nodded her head, still grinning. "That was a good one," she clucked, reaching for her hairbrush. "A really good one."

7

Serafine arrived in early July with a hundred synthetic platinum braids dangling down her back like tentacles. The natural brown of her eyes was camouflaged behind emerald-green contacts. A short, plump black American friend named Didi accompanied her. The lobes of Didi's ears were double-pierced and a diamond stud twinkled in her left nostril.

Serafine brought gifts for the children: designer clothing for Agwe and two videos for Abeo—*Watership Down* and *The Wizard of Oz*—as well as a genuine US-cooked McDonald's Big Mac hamburger that she had covered in layers of Saran wrap and tinfoil for the journey. The bread was soggy and the meat cold, but Abeo gobbled it down anyway. When she was done, a mayonnaise-glazed smile spread across her lips.

After dinner, the family piled into the living room to watch *The Wizard of Oz*. Abeo was fascinated by the movie—she barely made a peep the entire time—and when it was done, she applauded with great vigor.

If not for Serafine's visit, Ismae would have remained in the guest room until Wasik banished his mother back to Prama.

But despite their differences, Wasik and Ismae

agreed to call a truce—at least while Serafine was in town.

So Ismae returned to their marriage bed.

That night, when Wasik reached for her, Ismae did not refuse him. Their lovemaking went on for hours. The following morning, their night of passion could not be concealed. Ismae wasn't just glowing, she was absolutely pulsing with light.

For the next few weeks, Abeo essentially became a tourist in her own country, seeing it through Didi's American eyes and experiencing it as she did.

It was only on the rarest of occasions that Abeo took public transportation—her father drove the family everywhere. So to Abeo, riding in the colorful, dilapidated minibuses known as *tro-tros* was as thrilling as an amusement park ride.

Day after day, the trio, hands linked, left the Kata homestead and headed toward the commercial district where Serafine waved down a *tro-tro* and the three happily crammed themselves in alongside people and livestock. One time Didi found herself sitting next to a woman who held an irate chicken in her lap and it pecked Didi from the time they climbed on until they got off.

On a cloudy Thursday morning, Abeo, Serafine, and Didi boarded a bus that took them across the border into Ghana and on to Accra.

Abeo had visited Ghana just twice in her young life. The first time was when she was barely a year old. Her parents had taken her by car to attend the wedding of a family friend. She was too young to remember the trip, but there was an album full of photos of Abeo, cradled in her mother's arms, grinning into the camera; all gums and cheeks, adorned in a gold-and-purple dress, her bald head wrapped in a matching head tie.

The second time she was six years old. She and Ismae had traveled to Ghana in the church van, along with other members of their congregation, to have a day of prayer and celebration with an affiliate house of worship in Accra. The trip had been long and hot. They rode with the windows down, fanning themselves with handkerchiefs and church programs. The van was old; it coughed black smoke, sat low to the ground, and was in need of new shocks. The driver had a gift for sighting potholes, but not avoiding them. When someone needed to urinate, they had to do so in the scrub that bounded either side of the road.

Now, in the air-conditioned coach, complete with a tiny bathroom, Abeo peered out at the rolling green savanna, bouncing her leg with excitement, half listening to Didi who was babbling at warp speed, jumping from one subject to the next, pausing only to flip through the pages of her guidebook. Serafine, the sponged headphones of her Walkman covering her ears, spent the three-hour journey bopping her head to the music of Shalamar, Khalif, and Mtume.

At Black Star Square, Abeo posed for a picture beneath Independence Arch. On a trip to the W.E.B. DuBois Centre, in the sitting room of the former home of the great thinker, Didi turned to the crowd of mostly white tourists and bellowed dramatically: *"One ever feels his two-ness—an American, a Negro; two souls, two thoughts, two reconciled strivings; two warring ideals in one dark body, whose dogged strength alone keeps it from being torn asunder!"*

Serafine flashed an apologetic smile at the visitors who stood staring.

Abeo giggled into her palms.

Serafine caught Didi by the wrist and dragged her away from the buzzing crowd. "What the hell was that?"

Didi smiled sheepishly. "Girl, DuBois's spirit must have jumped on me," she giggled. "These white folk need to know!" And with that she threw a wink at Abeo, who was still laughing.

At the Kwame Nkrumah Mausoleum and Memorial Park, erected in memory of Osagyefo (the Messiah) Dr. Kwame Nkrumah, the first president of Ghana, Abeo was struck mute by the structure—where the bodies of the great leader and his wife were laid to rest. She listened in awe as the tour guide explained that the design was meant to represent the Akan culture's symbol of peace—an upside-down sword. She was equally enchanted by the magnificent golden fountains in the park.

At the Tetteh Quarshie Art Market, Didi haggled over the price of a wooden sculpture of a naked man seated on a tree limb. Serafine covered Abeo's eyes when she saw her staring at the penis.

With each stop they made, Didi shared small nuggets of knowledge. In the marketplace, she pointed to a bolt of colorful cloth stamped with a running motif of diamonds encased in rectangular boxes. "See this, Abeo? This cloth is from the Ivory Coast, from a town called Korhogo—"

"It is?" Serafine cut in, stepping over to examine the fabric herself. "How do you know that?"

Didi ignored Serafine, extended her hand, and ran the tip of her finger along the geometric design. "This represents the talking drum," she informed Abeo.

"Talking drum?" Abeo batted her eyes in confusion.

"The *lunna!*" Serafine cried with delight. "Heh," she laughed, "at least I do know that!"

"Yes, you're right, Serafine, it is the *lunna* drum," Didi confirmed.

Abeo brought her ear close to the material, closed her eyes, and listened, but all she heard was the busy Accra traffic blaring all around her like white noise. "I don't hear any drum," she sighed, her voice dripping with disappointment.

"You don't?" Didi's eyes twinkled mischievously. She bent over Abeo, pressing her own ear to the material. Her face tensed with concentration. "I hear it. Maybe you have to listen a little bit harder."

Abeo's eyes stretched.

"Go on," Didi coaxed, "try again."

Once again, Abeo closed her eyes. The shopkeeper, an inky-colored man with a line-thin mustache, eyed them with great amusement from behind his wooden counter.

Abeo pressed her ear firmly against the fabric. Soon, the blare of horns, screeching tires, and cries of street vendors hawking their wares began to fade, and for one crystal moment there was nothing but silence. And then a faint sound echoed in the hush. Abeo wrapped her arms around the bolt of fabric, pushed her ear deeper into the material. The faint beat of a lone drum reverberated in her ear; the sound gradually swelled until it seemed her entire body throbbed. Surprised and shaken, Abeo snatched her head away and turned startled eyes on Didi.

"Did you hear it?"

A speechless, shaken Abeo could do little more than nod her head.

That Sunday the entire family attended church—well, all but Grandmother, who refused to because she claimed a white god was no god of hers—where Abeo made her First Communion. She looked like an angel in her white dress and matching patent-leather shoes. For the occasion, Ismae had taken Abeo to the hairdresser, where Abeo grinned all through the wash, dry, press, and curl.

At the church, Ismae welled with pride as she watched Abeo prepare to take, for the first time in her life, the body of Christ. Ismae squeezed Wasik's hand, but when he didn't squeeze back in response, she looked over at him to find that he was staring down into his lap, his face void of emotion.

Abeo stood tall and proud before the priest with the palms of her small hands pressed tightly together. The priest used the thin wafer to make the sign of the cross over her head and then held the wafer inches from her lips, announcing with great reverence, "The body of Christ."

Abeo responded, "Amen," closed her eyes, opened her mouth, and presented her tongue.

Ismae had wanted to give Abeo a party to celebrate the special occasion, but to her surprise and Wasik's relief, their daughter declined. "I'd rather go to the beach," she said.

And so she and the family spent the entire day at Laleb Beach, running through the surf until their fingers were wrinkled. Afterward, they filled their bellies with sausage and fish kebabs. The adults drank beer after beer while Abeo glugged down three bottles of orange soda.

They stayed until the sun changed from daffodil to ruby and drained into the sea. Bonfires were lit, amateur acrobats cartwheeled and tumbled their way up and down the sandy shoreline, people sang, and the stars floated a little bit closer to the earth.

8

The following week, Serafine talked Wasik into driving them to the Cape Coast of Ghana for an overnight stay. "It's important that Didi visits the slave castle," Serafine pushed when Wasik began to make excuses.

They invited Grandmother, but she clucked her tongue. "What I want to go there for?"

The normally three-hour drive took four and a half hours. A truck carrying diesel fuel had overturned, blocking traffic for miles. On top of that, it seemed to Wasik that all of the black Americans visiting Ghana had chosen that day to make the trip to the place that had made their descendants orphans in their own land.

When he expressed this, followed by a smug laugh, Didi made a sound in her throat, admonishing him through clenched teeth that she didn't think slavery was a joking matter.

Wasik mumbled an apology and turned the volume up on the radio to conceal his humiliation.

Abeo stared out the back window watching the chaos of Port Masi fade. The traffic eventually thinned and Wasik was able to accelerate, racing past burgundy hills, rows and rows of cotton and pineapple fields, savannas dotted with orange and cacao trees.

Serafine closed her eyes and fell asleep. Abeo and Didi remained awake, chattering like excited sparrows.

Halfway through their journey, Abeo lowered her window and waved at a line of children marching single file, singing and swinging their long dark arms. The kids smiled and waved back.

The traffic came to a halt at the foot of a drawbridge that had been raised over a trickle of a river.

Hawkers swarmed the still vehicles, peddling everything from food to jumper cables, baseball caps, and plastic shopping bags from high-end Western department stores. Wasik lowered the driver's-side window and the Ghanaian heat rushed in, smothering the air-conditioned chill of the car. He summoned a girl barely older than Abeo, who was carrying a tray of one-man thousand—fingernail-sized fish—fried to a golden crisp.

He purchased five bags and five bottles of water, which he distributed among his wife and the family.

The drawbridge was lowered and the traffic ebbed forward.

In no time, the scenery changed yet again. The roadside shanty shops, gargantuan anthills, and clusters of desiccated bush soon gave way to a sandy beach and a procession of coconut trees that were so tall, their palms seemed to brush the bottom of the sky. Beyond the trees were the cresting waves of the sapphire Atlantic Ocean.

Wasik cut off the air conditioner and pressed the lever that magically lowered all four windows, instantly flooding the car with an aromatic mixture of banana and coconut.

They'd reserved a modest four-bedroom, two-bath, split-level guesthouse a block from the beach. The structure had once been a gem, but was now slowly slipping into disrepair. The faucets leaked, the hardwood floors squeaked, and the mattresses were thin and stiff, but the location was beautiful—everywhere they turned offered a panoramic view of the sea.

They had dinner at a small restaurant where the owner seated them at a table that looked out over the water. They enjoyed a sumptuous meal beneath an evening sky swimming with purple clouds.

Serafine and Didi reminisced over bottles of wine, recounting their sordid adventures in New York.

"Remember him? He was the one with the long . . ." Serafine raised her finger to her lips and nodded in Abeo's direction.

Didi winked. "A loooooong nose. He had a very, very long nose!" Serafine, Didi, and Ismae dissolved in girlish giggles.

Wasik cleared his throat disapprovingly and lifted the sleeping Agwe from the high chair. "It's getting late," he grumbled, "I think we should head back to the house and put the children to bed."

Didi placed her hand over the check. "Let me take care of this."

"Oh no, we couldn't," Ismae wailed. "You are our guest and you've spent so much money on Abeo, taking her out and buying her gifts—"

Didi raised her hand. "Please, you have been such gracious hosts. Opening your home to me, treating me like family. I am so very grateful. Please, let me do this one small thing."

Wasik's shoulders slumped with relief. When Didi and Serafine first raised the idea of an overnight excursion to the coast, he had no clue Ismae would want to tag along. When she made her intentions known, Wasik didn't feel he could ask her not to. Worse yet, he'd said: "Why don't we make it a family affair? A minivacation of sorts. I could use a break from Port Masi."

Even as the words hung in the air, Wasik was regretting them. They were broke. Piss-poor, truth be told. Their savings account was empty and they were living off the kindness of his brother who was a successful gynecologist in London. But family or not, Wasik knew that this charity would soon come to an end.

Ismae had no idea they were living on borrowed money, and Wasik would do everything he could to keep her in the dark.

Ismae threw her arm over Didi's shoulders. "How else are we supposed to treat you? Hospitality is the African way," she laughed.

"Thank you," Wasik said, hoisting Agwe onto his shoulder. He gave Ismae an expectant look, but she diverted her eyes, so he turned his attention to Abeo. "Come on, young lady, I think it's getting very close to your bedtime."

Abeo frowned, opened her mouth to protest, but closed it again when Wasik's warm eyes turned to ice.

"Well, we're going to stay awhile. Maybe even have another bottle of wine," Serafine chuckled as she turned over the empty bottle and watched a single scarlet droplet fall onto the green tablecloth.

"I'm going to stay too," Ismae announced in a small voice.

Wasik rose from the table. "Okay, I'll see you back at the house."

* * *

The next day they got an early start. Wasik planned to drop the women at the castle and return for them later.

"I'll stay with the children, take them to the beach," he said over breakfast.

Abeo's head bounced up. "I'm not going to the slave castle?"

"No," Wasik answered without looking up from his plate.

Ismae wrinkled her nose. "But why, Wasik?"

When he raised his head, all eyes were on him. He set his fork down. "I-I just think she's too young for all of that . . . that . . ." He couldn't seem to lasso the right word, so he repeated, "I just think she's too young."

Abeo's lower lip trembled with disappointment. Didi had told her so much about the Africans who were taken to America and turned into slaves, how important it was that she—that all of them—visit the place where it all began and ended for millions of men, women, and children.

"Oh, Abeo," Didi had sadly moaned, "you have no idea how many of your own ancestors, people who share your bloodline, were sold away from their lives."

Abeo hadn't understood some of it—the bloodline and the idea that one person could own another—but even at her young age, Didi's sentimentality was not lost on her.

Didi had continued: "Imagine if you were taken away from your mother and father, never to see them again. How would that make you feel?"

"Sad."

"Right, well, it's the same for black Americans. Imagine Africa as the mother and father of black Americans; a mother and father who they knew they had but never met. Imagine that one day they have the opportunity to meet them, to be reunited. How do you think that would make them feel?"

Abeo had thought about it for a moment. Her eyes lit up when she piped, "Happy!"

"Exactly."

She had to go to the slave castle. "Papa, pleeeee-aaaasssse," Abeo wailed.

"Oh, Wasik," Ismae offered gently, "let her come. I think she's mature enough to handle it."

Wasik released an agitated sigh. He couldn't win for losing with Ismae. He would be happy when Agwe was old enough to help balance the sheet. "Okay," he acquiesced.

"And you should come as well," Didi interjected. "It's your history too."

Wasik smirked at her. He'd never visited the castle. And if he'd ever harbored a desire to do so, it had been crushed long ago by the warnings and terrifying ghost stories of his elders. But now he was grown: a husband, father, and provider for his family. He received Didi's words not as an invitation, but a challenge.

"But of course," Wasik responded, as if he'd planned to come all along.

Ismae's eyebrows rose. "Well, who will watch Agwe?"

Wasik glanced at their toddler. "Uhm . . ." he started, absently scratching his chin. "I guess we can leave him with Mama Tati?"

It wasn't the worst idea in the world. Mama Tati was

the domestic charged with cleaning and cooking for the visitors at the guesthouse.

On the low side of sixty, rotund, and pleasant, Mama Tati had been in the employ of several homeowners for two decades. She was loved and trusted by her employers and guests and often took on responsibilities that fell outside of her standard duties. Babysitting was just one of those chores.

Ismae nodded. "I guess that would be okay."

As they approached by car, Elmina Castle emerged from the horizon like a dream. Its whitewashed walls pressed against the indigo sky, casting shadows over the bucking Atlantic Ocean.

They fell quiet as Wasik eased the car into a parking space and cut the engine. Abeo was confused by the silence—not just the absence of conversation, but the weight of it.

Didi was the first out of the car. She stood on unsteady legs, gazing apprehensively at the imposing structure.

"Didi?" Serafine called out, pointing at the kidney bean–shaped bulge on the underside of Didi's left jaw.

Didi touched her index finger to the swollen flesh. "Oh, this?" She shrugged. "Nerves."

"What's there to be nervous about?" Abeo ventured, perplexed.

Didi thought for a moment. "You see, baby," she cooed, smoothing her palm across Abeo's plaits, "my great-great-grandparents were slaves. I don't know if they were born in America or stolen from Africa. They could have come from Ukemby or Ghana. They might have even been held in this very prison . . ."

It was the first time Abeo had heard the castle referred to as a prison.

Didi shivered with emotion. "Families ripped apart," she mumbled, turning her attention back to the castle, "never to see one another again." She swiped a fat wet tear from her cheek.

Abeo wasn't so sure she wanted to go into the castle prison anymore.

Wasik, who had been standing off to the side, suddenly stepped to Abeo, took her by the hand, and gently pulled her to his hip. All of this talk about slavery and broken families was making him uneasy. "Are we going in or what?" he barked. He'd not meant to sound harsh, but it was out and he couldn't take it back. He met the women's stupefied gazes with his own apologetic one.

"Wasik, when did you become so insensitive?" Serafine admonished.

Once inside, Wasik trailed behind, stepping cautiously as if the ground were covered with broken glass.

They stopped to take photos beside the ancient rusting cannons that extended out over the ocean like reaching arms. Nearby, a group of black women holding hands belted out a tearful song in a language Abeo did not understand. To her left, an elderly white couple made the sign of the cross over their hearts before tossing a dozen yellow roses over the wall, into the water. A few feet away, a young Asian woman collapsed to the ground and wept openly.

Eventually, Abeo and her family joined a dozen other people for a tour of the castle. Their guide was a tall, dark man named Morris who had lived his entire life on the Cape Coast and had never ventured into the country's interior. The group followed him down the narrow stairway into the first dungeon, where Morris abruptly switched off his flashlight, throwing them into darkness. Abeo yelped in surprise and wrapped her arms around Serafine's waist.

"More than two hundred Africans were imprisoned in this very chamber for months at a time," Morris explained in a low, ominous voice. "We are a small fraction of that number and you cannot shift one inch without touching your neighbor."

Abeo tested his claim and the truth terrified her.

"The separation of families began right here, long before they reached the shores of America, Europe, Brazil, and the Caribbean islands. The jailers mixed Ga-Adangbe people with Abron and Adele with Bimoba, and Ukemban with Chumburung—so that there would be no possibility of communication, hence no threat of revolt."

The crowd shifted uncomfortably. Wasik wiped at the perspiration forming on his neck and forehead. The darkness was clawing. He willed Morris to switch on the flashlight, and after a few more excruciating moments, the yellow beam sliced through the darkness and landed on a rectangular opening in the wall high above their heads.

"Food was thrown down to the captives from that hole." Morris swung the beam to another opening, this one square, the size of box, a tiny box, one small enough to hold a single teacup or bottle of expensive perfume. Once again, Morris switched off the flashlight.

The opening was so small that not one of them could make out the blue sky or the lingering yellow sun. So minute that not even the daylight could trickle in; it just rested on the lip of the cavity, glowing like a flawed diamond.

"That is all of the natural light they were allowed," Morris continued.

Abeo glanced over her shoulder but couldn't make out the look on her father's face in the darkness. Wasik stood completely still, staring, gnawing his lower lip.

Morris switched on the flashlight and aimed the beam at the uneven floor beneath their feet. "Do you know what this is?" he questioned. "Do you know what you are standing on?"

Abeo studied the ground. It looked like mud, like shiny hardened mud.

A lone voice cried out, "Stones? Old stones?"

"Yes, old stones, as well as centuries of calcified blood, bone, flesh, and excrement."

The crowd groaned. Abeo did not understand the words *excrement* or *calcified*, but she did understand blood and bones and closed her eyes, because she did not want to see those things in the cobbled floor.

Wasik's stomach lurched. He suspected he was treading perilously close to bringing up his breakfast.

The group moved on to the various dungeons that once held the weaker men, women, and children.

"Children too?" Abeo asked Ismae, who responded with a slow, sad nod.

The final room they entered was dungeon number five, where those Africans who were ready for export had been kept. Back then, Morris told them, the dungeon emptied into a tunnel, which led to the exit now famously known as the Door of No Return. The mouth of the tunnel had long since been sealed, and an Ashanti shrine had been erected in its place—which was guarded night and day by an Ashanti priest. Visitors to dungeon number five paid homage to those Africans who had passed through the tunnel centuries ago by leaving offerings of fruit, flowers, and money.

After the group had placed their own offerings before the priest, they formed a circle. Hands linked, they stood somberly listening to their thudding hearts.

Didi's voice was the first to splinter the silence: "I think we should pray."

Moaning their agreement, the circle of people bowed their heads.

Didi began: "Dear Lord, we send up prayers to our brothers and sisters who passed through this place so many years ago. We are grateful for their sacrifices and we pray that we can adequately take the knowledge and the spirit that we've gained here back to those people who may never be able to make this pilgrimage. We ask that You forgive those hands that were bloodied with this inhumane and horrendous act and also that we all learn from this lesson and go forward declaring, *Never, ever again*. Amen."

By the end of the prayer, a number of people were weeping.

Ismae squeezed Abeo's hand. "You okay, baby?"

Abeo was not okay. She felt a great sorrow in her chest and it hurt like hell.

"It's okay to cry." Ismae pulled Abeo into her. Wasik came and rested his hands on Abeo's shoulders. Ismae looked into his wet eyes and felt the love she held for him roll through her like a wave.

Back outside, back in the salt-tinged air, hands still tightly clasped, they marched solemnly along the cobblestoned alleyway toward the Door of No Return.

The solid double wooden doors stood at least ten feet tall. The height and width of them was imposing to young Abeo, but that is not what caused her body to quake as it did. What struck fear into her young heart was the history that lay beyond the wooden panels and brass hardware. You see, Morris had revived history and little Abeo was finding it hard to distinguish between the now and what had been. Morris reached for the door handle and Abeo's breath caught in her throat. She ordered her eyes to close, but they refused, and so she braced herself for the vision of a ship bobbing on the ocean, its deck teeming with shackled human cargo.

Ismae, sensing the girl's trepidation, lifted her into her arms, whispering, "It's okay, Abeo, don't be afraid."

Morris pushed the doors open and they walked out into the bright sun. Strewn across the topaz-colored Atlantic were nearly two dozen fishing boats, their masts wrapped in colorful cloth. On the shore were just as many children, happily kicking about seashells and soccer balls. Abeo breathed a sigh of relief.

Didi, Serafine, and Wasik stood before the doors with their heads tilted back on their necks. Ismae followed their eyes to the wooden sign that hung above the doorway.

Ismae pulled Abeo tighter to her chest. "Can you read what that says, baby?"

"*Door. Of. No. Return*," Abeo replied.

9

The days that followed the visit to Elmina Castle were solemn ones. The weather turned foul—storm clouds blotted out the sun and rain fell for three straight days.

Didi's and Serafine's moods mirrored the weather. They spent those damp days on the back veranda sipping beer, counting raindrops, and smoking cigarettes. When Abeo tried to engage them in a game of checkers or suggested they put on music and dance, Serafine sent her away with a quiet word and a quick wave of her hand.

Bored one afternoon, Abeo wandered into the room that Serafine and Didi shared and amused herself by sifting through their belongings. She discovered an American nickel lodged behind the tongue of one of Serafine's sneakers. From the zipper pocket of Didi's cosmetics bag Abeo fished out four square blue packets with the word *Trojan* stamped across the front.

Perfume bottles, bobby pins, lotions, and various pieces of jewelry were scattered across the top of the dresser. Abeo examined each item. She slipped the red bangles on her wrists and held the dangling gold earrings up to her earlobes. She placed rings on each of her ten fingers, stood in front of the mirror, raised her hands to her face, and wiggled her fingers until she giggled.

One ring was especially beautiful. It had a wide silver band and an oval-shaped, powder-blue stone that was marbled with fine white lines. It reminded her of the heaven she'd seen in a book that showed Michelangelo's *The Creation of Adam*.

Abeo slipped the ring into her pocket.

Days later at the airport, Didi and Serafine hugged Abeo and her parents goodbye.

For some reason, Abeo felt sadder than she had in the past when Serafine's time with them had come to a close.

"Don't do this to me, Abeo," Serafine said as the crying Abeo clung to her. "Don't make me weep in public." Serafine peeled her off. "Next summer will be here before you know it."

"Can't you come for Christmas, Auntie?"

"I tell you this: if I win the lottery I will come for Christmas, okay?"

"Okay," Abeo sniffed.

Every night Abeo slipped the stolen ring onto her finger and prayed for Serafine to win the lottery, even though she had no idea what a lottery was.

10

asik looked around and swore that he could hear his life collapsing. Every day it changed—some days it sounded like a falling tree, other times an avalanche of rocks. On that particular day, however, it boomed, cracked, and shuddered like a twister bearing down on him. Wasik nearly jumped out of his skin with fright. He was sure the sky had fallen. He crept to the window and peeked out—the sky was still firmly in place, so he was convinced his mind was coming apart.

A day later a water pipe broke in the house, the roof began to leak, and the alternator on the Mercedes sputtered and died. And to make matters worse, the home occupied by the man who was conducting the investigation of Wasik burned to the ground and turned everything into cinder: the gentleman's clothes, his furniture, his family photos, and the file on Wasik Kata. The investigation would have to restart from scratch. The newspapers had a field day. One journalist asked a simple question: *In this age of photocopy machines, why?* The story made the front page.

Wasik was devastated. He developed a tic above his right eye and his afternoon drinking now began just before noon. On top of everything else, Agwe fell sick.

The doctor said, "Don't worry, it's just a cold," and prescribed antibiotics. But the cold turned into pneumonia and Agwe was soon hospitalized.

Grandmother stared at Wasik, the question on her face clear as crystal: *How much more before you believe?*

One night, Wasik went to Abeo's room, knocked on the door, and pushed it open before she could respond. He walked in to find her seated on the bed, dressed in her nightgown, a book open on her lap, the stolen ring hidden beneath her pillow.

"Hello, Papa," she smiled.

"Hello, Abeo." Wasik pulled the door closed behind him. "What are you reading?"

"*Little Red Riding Hood.*"

"Again?" Wasik laughed.

"I like it," Abeo grinned.

Wasik turned his eyes to the poster on the wall. "Michael Jackson," he said. "I was a Michael Jackson fan once, but that was when he was a little boy and was singing with his brothers. Now he's a solo artist with a silver glove." He laughed again and then did something completely out of character: he raised himself up onto his toes, rapidly shook one hand, and screeched, "*Beat it, just beat it!*"

Abeo covered her mouth and giggled. "Papa! You look silly!"

"I suppose I do." The humor in his smile faded. "I-I wish that I could . . . I mean I wish that he was coming to Ukemby to perform. I would take you for your birthday."

Abeo folded her hands on top of the book, her smile widened.

Wasik licked his lips and glanced nervously around the room. "Well, since I can't deliver Michael Jackson, tell me what you would like for your birthday."

Abeo shot Wasik a quizzical look. It was an odd request; her birthday was months away. She shrugged her shoulders. "I don't know, Papa."

"Oh?" Wasik seemed surprised. "Well, I guess you can think about it and let me know."

Abeo fiddled with pages of her book. "Okay."

Wasik ran his hands through his hair. "You know, Abeo, your mother and I love you very much. You know that, don't you?"

"Yes."

"And do you love us?"

"Yes, Papa."

"We would do anything for you, you know that, right?"

"Yes, Papa."

"And would you do anything for us?"

The question made Abeo feel uncomfortable. "Yes," she mumbled.

He offered her a weak smile. "Good, good. It's late, let's get you tucked in."

11

The pressures continued to mount.

The car was in the repair shop collecting dust, but Wasik couldn't spare the money to get it out. Without a car, Ismae had to take the *tro-tro* to the market and anyplace else she needed or wanted to go. He did manage to get the water pipe repaired—a plumber friend owed him a favor—and Wasik had done his best on the roof with hammer, nails, and a slab of wood, but the water still found a way in; so now the ceiling in their bedroom looked like a piss-stained mattress.

Wasik waited for things to get better. One week passed, then two, three, and four. His problems followed him into the next month and the month after that. He borrowed more money from his brother.

Grandmother said, "Your family is suffering. You go to *that* church and pray to *that* god, but what does he do for you? Nothing!"

Wasik balled his fists in anger. His mother was right, but Ismae had made it quite clear that she didn't agree.

Grandmother was well aware of Ismae's opposition. She straightened her back, cleared her throat, and spoke to her son through clenched teeth: "You are the man of this house, the husband, the head of this family, the decision maker. Don't worry about her. She is the wife, the mother of your children. It is her place to walk behind you, not ahead of you and not beside you."

That night the rain came down in torrents and Wasik lay wide awake in bed listening to the *plink-plink-plink* of the water dripping into the metal bucket Ismae had placed beneath the leak.

Plink-plink-plink.

He turned over and pulled the pillow over his head, but the sound permeated the material.

Plink-plink-plink.

Wasik tossed the pillow to the floor and glared at Ismae's sleeping face. How could he have married such a defiant woman?

Plink-plink-plink.

He was the man. He was the *man*. He was the man of this house!

Plink-plink-plink.

What he says goes!

Plink-plink-plink.

The sound was driving him mad. He got up and went into the living room. It followed him there. He went into the kitchen and there it was . . . *plink-plink-plink* . . .

He pressed his fingers into his ears and began to recite the Lord's Prayer: "*Our Father, who art in heaven . . .*"

PLINK. PLINK. PLINK.

Finally, Wasik flung his hands up to the heavens and bellowed: "I WILL put other gods before You because You have left me no choice!"

Plink.

Wasik tiptoed into Abeo's room and shook her awake.

"Papa?" Abeo yawned, rubbing her eyes.

"Abeo, get up, we have to go," he whispered.

"Go where? Where is Mama?"

"Stop asking questions and do as I say." The sternness in his voice snapped Abeo fully awake. Wasik reached into the closet, pulled out a dress, and threw it at her. "Put this on. Hurry."

He'd called a neighbor, made up a story about an emergency, and asked to borrow their Toyota. He practically shoved Abeo into the backseat. The owner had dogs that he carted around like children, so the car was filled with hair that tickled her nose and immediately brought on a wave of sneezes.

Either Wasik didn't notice or didn't care, because he didn't even say, *God bless you, Abeo.* He just released the hand brake, shifted the gear into neutral, and coasted the car silently down the driveway and onto the street.

"But Papa, it's so late. Where are we going?"

Wasik clenched his jaw, placed the car in drive, hit the lights, and stepped on the accelerator.

Abeo got on her knees and stared out the back window. The last person she saw was Grandmother standing in the doorway, her arms long and stiff at her sides, her face blank.

A siren went off in Abeo's head and her eyes filled with tears. "Where are we going?" she blubbered. "Where's Mama?"

"Just be quiet," Wasik ordered thinly. "Just sit there and be quiet."

Nearly two hours passed before Wasik pulled the car onto a lonely dirt road, stopped, jumped out, and disappeared into the bush without a word. A terrified Abeo curled herself into a ball and watched the night for monsters.

Wasik soon returned, accompanied by a bent old man who glanced briefly at Abeo before pointing in the direction they'd come. Wasik thanked him, climbed back into the car, turned the vehicle around, and sped off.

Horrible thoughts streaked through Abeo's mind. Had she done something wrong and this was some type of punishment? Yet she dared not ask, because although the man driving the car looked like her father, she believed him to be an impostor.

The road slowly transformed into a corridor of rocks and ditches that jostled the Toyota angrily on its shocks. The black night was receding into a gray morning when Abeo spied women walking along the road balancing baskets and large bowls atop their heads. Some had babies bound to their backs with cloth. An old woman using a fallen tree limb as a staff raised an arthritic hand in greeting just as a goat ran out into the road. Wasik swerved wildly, successfully avoiding the goat, but not the four-foot-tall termite mound.

"Are you okay?" he asked the whimpering Abeo.

After taking a moment to check the Toyota for damages, he eased the car back onto the road, driving cautiously for the next ten or so miles before stopping in front of a large mud hut in the middle of a valley lush with vegetation.

A woman stepped from the hut and eyed Wasik expectantly. When she spotted Abeo trembling in the backseat, a faint smile surfaced on her lips.

"Stay here," Wasik instructed.

Outside of the car, beneath the brightening sky, Wasik and the woman exchanged some words before he went into the hut. The woman adjusted her head wrap, sauntered over to the vehicle, peered in at Abeo, and tapped the window the way one would the glass of an aquarium.

Wasik reappeared, opened the trunk, and pulled out a sack packed with pots, cooking utensils, and three bottles of schnapps. He handed the sack to the woman, who thanked him before setting it on the ground.

Wasik rounded the car and opened the back door. "Get out, Abeo," he ordered without looking at her.

Abeo shook her head and scurried to the far side of the seat.

Wasik sucked his teeth in frustration, reached into the car, caught Abeo by the collar of her dress, and yanked her savagely from the vehicle.

"Please, Papa, please!" Abeo begged as he shoved her into the bracing arms of the woman.

Wasik never once met her confused and terrified gaze, nor did he say goodbye, he just climbed into the Toyota and pulled away.

"Papa, Papa!" she shouted, but Wasik kept driving.

Abeo screamed until the woman slapped her across the mouth. "Stop your crying and fussing. You should be honored to be here, to become *trokosi*, to become the wife of the gods."

It was 1985; Abeo was nine years, seven months, and three days old.

12

When Ismae opened her eyes, the room was bathed in bright morning light. The clock on the nightstand read 8:45. Ismae couldn't remember the last time she had slept past six.

Her eyes moved to the crib and when she saw that Agwe wasn't there, she panicked. She leaped from the bed, rushed to the closed bedroom door, yanked it open, and nearly ran smack into Grandmother, who was standing there with Agwe planted on her hip. She'd reached for the knob just as the door opened and her hand remained suspended in midair as she and Ismae stared at each other in surprise.

"Oh, you're up?" Grandmother said.

Agwe stretched his arms out to Ismae.

"He was hungry and wet," Grandmother continued as she passed Agwe to his mother. "You didn't hear him crying, so I took care of it."

"Where's Wasik?" Ismae asked, carefully examining Agwe.

Grandmother was smug; she shrugged her shoulders, turned, and walked away.

Ismae followed. "Where's Abeo?"

"Where else would she be but at school?"

Two o'clock came and went and Wasik still hadn't called or returned home. Ismae stood on the front veranda scanning the faces of the schoolchildren who filed past her house. She caught sight of Abeo's friend Poppy walking by, laughing with a group of girls. "Poppy, Poppy!" she called, waving her over. "Where is Abeo?"

Poppy gave Ismae a strange look. "I thought she was home sick."

"Sick?"

"She didn't come to school today, so I thought she was sick."

Ismae's stomach lurched.

Back in the house, Ismae stormed into the kitchen where she found Grandmother seated at the table sipping hot tea. When Grandmother looked up, Ismae saw the truth in her eyes. Ismae slapped the cup from her hand, sending it hurtling to the floor, where it shattered.

Grandmother raised her arms protectively over her face.

Ismae screamed, "Bitch!"

"It is for the best, you will see," the old woman stammered.

It was dark when Wasik finally came home. Grandmother greeted him at the front door, took him by the hand, and guided him into the dining room.

"Does she know?" he whispered.

Grandmother set a plate of pounded cassava and oxtail stew down before him. "Yes."

Wasik pushed the plate away. His stomach was in knots. "I can't eat."

"But you must."

Wasik's shoulders slumped with grief. "What have I done?"

Grandmother patted his back. "You have done the right thing, the honorable thing, for your family."

Wasik pushed himself up from the table. "I have to go and talk to her. I have to explain . . ."

Grandmother tugged at his wrist. "Sit, eat." Wasik shrugged her off. "Wait, I have to tell you . . ."

Wasik walked away from her words. When he reached the bedroom, he took a deep breath before pushing the door open. The bed was neatly made, the curtains drawn, his slippers waited alone at the edge of the carpet. The top of the dresser was empty save for his bottle of cologne and a hairbrush. Scrawled across the mirror in Ismae's crimson lipstick were the words: I hate you!

She was gone.

His mother's voice sounded behind him: "Don't worry, she will be back."

It had taken all the strength Ismae had to keep from curling her fingers around Grandmother's throat. Instead, she had called her names and damned both her and Wasik to hell.

Through a deluge of blinding tears, Ismae packed a few belongings into two suitcases and taken a taxi to the middle-class neighborhood of Braka, where her cousin Thema lived with her husband Joseph and daughter Ebony.

"Ismae?" Joseph was surprised to see her and the baby. He peered over her shoulder, fully expecting to see Wasik's Mercedes parked on the street. He opened his mouth to question her unannounced visit and then saw the suitcases—and thought better of it.

"Come in, come in," he said.

"Who is it, Joseph?" Thema appeared behind him, her hands wrapped in a dishtowel. "Ismae? Well, what a nice—" she started, and then stopped when she saw the wrecked state her cousin was in. Thema flung the towel over her shoulder and rushed to Ismae. "What has happened?"

Ismae's bottom lip trembled.

Thema turned to her husband. "Joseph, would you please put some tea on?"

"No tea. Do you have Guinness?"

Joseph and Thema exchanged surprised glances— Ismae was not a drinker.

"Okay then," Thema uttered slowly. "Joseph, bring us two bottles of Guinness."

In the living room Ismae set Agwe down on the floor and he quickly crawled off toward a potted plant.

"Ebony," Thema called to her daughter, "come and take care of little Agwe while your aunt and I talk."

They retired to the patio. The laughter of a talk show audience echoed from the television in a neighboring house. They settled in matching bamboo patio chairs.

Thema, short and round, folded one golden leg over the other, brought the bottle of Guinness to her lips, took a few sips, and then planted her gaze on Ismae's sad face. "Tell me," she urged.

Where should she begin? With Nsun and the van accident that killed the goats? The death of her father-in-law? The arrival of her mother-in-law? Wasik's suspension? Agwe's boils? Her broken ankle? Where?

Ismae began with the suspension and plowed through to the leaky roof. She didn't speak about Nsun and the goats—that just seemed too ridiculous to mention, even though it was central to the mess Grandmother and Wasik had created.

Thema listened attentively, and when Ismae was done, she patted her cousin's hand affectionately.

"All of these tears for a patch of bad luck?" Thema was relieved. "Oh, Ismae, you are much too sensitive. Things will turn around, they always do."

"That's not all of it," Ismae whispered.

"Oh?"

Ismae drained the bottle of Guinness, welcoming the icy trail the cold stout carved down her throat. She drew her palm across her forehead and shook the perspiration into the still air.

"He took her to become *trokosi*," she finally mumbled.

Thema blinked. Sure she'd heard wrong, she leaned closer to Ismae. "*He*? Took who?"

Ismae bit down on her lip until it sprang blood.

Thema pressed: "Who are you talking about, Ismae?"

"Wasik took . . ." She couldn't bear to say the unsayable. She breathed deep and blurted: "Wasik took Abeo to become *trokosi*."

Thema stared at her for one long moment. When she'd processed what Ismae had said, she gripped her cousin's hand and squeezed it so hard Ismae cried out. "You're mistaken, Ismae. He would not do such a thing."

Ismae pulled her hand away and melted into the chair. "But he did."

WIFE OF THE GODS

ZOLTA REGION, UKEMBY

1985—1999

13

After Wasik left Abeo at the shrine, the old woman took her to a one-room hut with two square windows and a dirt floor. The morning spilled in through spaces in the thatched roof that were in need of repair. A stool sat conspicuously in the center of the room. A gray garment, folded into a square, rested on the seat of the stool. On the floor against the wall was a bright yellow bucket and four grass mats stacked one on top of the other.

The woman clasped her hands behind her back and walked a slow circle around Abeo. When she was done, she pushed her fists into her thick hips, glowered down at the girl, and announced, "I am Mama Darkwa. What is your name?"

Abeo whispered her name.

"We do not go for any nonsense here, do you understand? You will do as you are told. And if you do otherwise, you will be punished."

Where was *here*? Abeo had no idea.

"Now, take off those clothes," Mama Darkwa ordered, slapping her across the head.

Abeo cried out and stumbled backward.

"Are you slow or just stupid? Have you already forgotten what I've just told you?"

Stunned, Abeo slowly slipped her dress over her head and placed it in the woman's waiting hand.

"Those too." Mama Darkwa wagged her finger at the undergarments she wore. Abeo hesitated for a half-second, but the sting of the blow to her head was still fresh, and so she quickly complied. Darkwa clucked her tongue and snatched the gold cross and chain from Abeo's neck. She held it up to the light and studied it briefly before tossing it to the ground and mashing it into the dirt with her foot.

"Come," Darkwa instructed after she'd retrieved the yellow bucket.

Abeo cupped her hands over her private area and followed the woman obediently out into the open. The sun was hot and the trees were alive with the chatter of birds. Eyes lowered with shame, Abeo stumbled along a path that wound between huts, through a thicket of brush, and ended at the bank of a wide river.

"Get in," Darkwa ordered.

The water was cold. Darkwa dumped bucket after bucket of icy water over Abeo's head until her body fell into spasms.

The woman pulled a bar of black soap from the pocket of her dress and raked it across Abeo's body, then slathered it through her hair until it was a foamy, woolly ball. She dropped the soap back into her pocket and pulled out a straight razor. When Abeo saw the blade, she began to shriek.

"Shut up!" Darkwa bellowed, using her middle and index fingers to pop Abeo across her lips. "Hold still or I might slip and cut off your ear."

Abeo held herself as rigid as possible while Darkwa

drew the blade expertly across her head, slicing off soapy locks that dropped into the water and were whisked away by the current.

When Darkwa was done she took Abeo back to the hut, where she pointed a long finger at the folded piece of fabric that rested on the stool: "Put that on."

It was a drab, sleeveless dress. She slipped it over her head, the rough material scratching her skin.

"Come," Darkwa commanded, and once again Abeo followed her from the hut. Now that she was clothed, she felt it safe to raise her eyes and survey her surroundings. Apparently, her father had left her in a small village that consisted of dozens of huts of various sizes. On the east side of the compound, a half-mile's walk from the huts, grew acres of corn. Abeo watched the tall stalks shudder beneath the swiftly moving hands of the young girls harvesting the produce. Beyond the corn was flat red earth, which gave way to mango trees, lush with fruit. Chicken coops and livestock holding pens flanked the southern side of the village. The river ran along the northern perimeter, hemmed in by a dark and imposing forest. The west, Abeo reasoned, must be the way out, the way home. They walked past lines of young bald girls carrying sacks and baskets, all outfitted in the same gray dress that Abeo now wore. Dangling from their necks were strings of crimson beads.

At the doorway of a very large hut, Darkwa gave Abeo a final once-over before shoving her inside. The hut had six windows, so it was bright with sunlight. In the center of the hut, surrounded by baskets of fruit and vegetables, sat an old man dressed in a white robe. Standing on either side of him were two girls, each fanning him with a massive palm leaf.

Abeo's eyes moved from the girls to the hanging folds of skin on the man's long face and finally down to his feet, which were bigger than any feet Abeo had ever seen outside of a cartoon. Not only were his feet enormous, but his toes seemed to be as long as his fingers. Abeo would have laughed if she wasn't so traumatized. He grinned at her, revealing a row of black teeth.

Darkwa knelt at the old man's feet and he presented his hand to her, which she kissed.

"This is Abeo Kata," she announced.

The priest nodded. "Come to me, my child."

Abeo's fear had drained down into her feet, turning them into cement. Darkwa reached around and tugged her forward.

"No need to be afraid," the man encouraged. Abeo stared at his finger toes. "How old are you?"

"Nine," she whispered.

"Do you know who I am?"

Abeo shook her head.

"I am the priest and this village is my shrine."

Abeo said nothing.

"Many years ago Yame came to me in a dream. Do you know who Yame is?"

Abeo shook her head again.

"Yame is the supreme god of heaven; the moon goddess and the sun god, the creator of sky, earth, and the underworld. Yame entered my body and informed me that I would represent him here on earth, that he would use me for the good of man; that I would be a *trokosi* priest and this village would be my shrine to him. I was twelve years old."

Abeo's face flushed with confusion.

"Do you know why you are here?"

Once again, Abeo shook her head.

"You are here to serve Yame. And in doing so, you will bring good fortune back to your family. You must be a very special little girl to be chosen by Yame to become his wife."

Abeo's eyes filled with tears. What was this old man saying to her? Wife? She was just nine years old. How could a child become a wife?

"You will follow the rules that Yame set forth, and in doing so, Yame will bless your family."

With that he nodded to Darkwa, who rose, walked over to the far wall of the hut, and pulled a blanket made of goatskin from a blue-and-yellow woven basket. This, she draped over the rounded shoulders of the priest. She returned to the basket and retrieved a white cloth, which she placed over Abeo's head, tying the loose ends into a knot at her throat. Darkwa forced Abeo to her knees, then went over to the table set against the opposite wall and retrieved a wooden smoking pipe with a long, sloped stem, which she lit and handed to the priest.

The old man chanted words that Abeo did not understand, sucked on the stem of the pipe, and blew a white stream of smoke into Abeo's face. The girl coughed, her eyes burned, and her head grew light. For an instant, she imagined her head lifting from her neck and floating off into the air like a balloon.

Darkwa slipped a rope of red beads around Abeo's neck.

The second stream of smoke the priest blew into

Abeo's face sent her cascading into unconsciousness.

When Abeo came to, she was stretched out on a floor mat, in yet another hut. She blinked at the blurry face hovering above her. "I'm Juba," the hazy image declared in a high-pitched voice.

Abeo winced at the spikes that the sound of Juba's voice drove into her brain. Slowly she gathered herself. Propped up on her elbows, Abeo glimpsed stick figures, numbers, and letters scrawled on the mud walls. Two young girls were seated on mats, hunched over bowls of food. A third girl was nursing an infant, even as her swollen belly jutted ominously out from her midsection.

"Are you hungry?" Juba asked.

Abeo tried to speak, but her tongue felt as heavy as wet cloth. So she shook her head. Juba sucked her teeth, scurried over to the window ledge, and retrieved a small gourd which she filled with granulated cassava—known as *gari*—from a clay pot on the floor near the door. Next to the pot was a bucket of water. Juba used her hands as a ladle, spooning the water from the bucket onto the *gari*. She brought the bowl to Abeo and offered it to her.

"Here," she said. "Stir it up and eat before it hardens."

Abeo stared down at the glop. *Gari* was not usually served alone, but accompanied by a rich meat or vegetable stew. Abeo glanced around at the other girls who were silently eating without complaint. She set her bowl down, lay back on the mat, and curled her knees to her chest.

"You must eat," Juba urged.

Abeo turned onto her side, squeezed her eyes shut, and waited for the terrible nightmare to come to an end.

After the other girls finished eating, they washed their bowls in the bucket and stacked them along the ledge of the window. The pregnant girl wrapped her baby on her back, walked over to Abeo, and nudged her with her toes. "Get up. We have to go to the fields."

Abeo didn't move.

"You, new girl. Come, before you cause big trouble," Juba pleaded from the doorway.

When Abeo still didn't move, the girls shrugged their shoulders and left. A few seconds later, Abeo was staring at the faded knees of denim jeans.

"Get up, you!"

His name was Duma and he was the oldest of the priest's sons. He also had the blackest heart of his eleven siblings. The *trokosi* girls secretly referred to him as The Evil One and *sasabonsam*: a vampire.

Tall, dark, and lanky, Duma had a flat nose that was so broad, it cast a perpetual shadow over his lips. His wide-set, slanted eyes imparted him with a serpentlike quality that matched his personality.

"You can sleep tonight," Duma growled. "Out to the fields, now!" He grabbed Abeo by her throat and yanked her to her feet. Abeo clawed at his hands but Duma held fast. He dragged her out of the cool hut, into the sweltering afternoon heat. Just when Abeo thought she would die from suffocation, he released his grip. "Walk," he commanded, shoving her down the dusty road and into the field.

There, amid stalks of corn, she was placed in the charge of the pregnant girl known as Nana.

Nana waited patiently for Abeo's sobs to dwindle to shuddering gasps before she spoke.

"Okay, new girl, pay attention." Nana wrapped her hand around an ear of corn. "Pierce the kernel with your thumbnail—if the juice runs milky, it's ready to be picked. If it looks like water, leave it." She grabbed hold of an ear, snapped her wrist sharply to the left, and pulled down. The corn came away from the stalk with a pop. "Now, you try it."

Her body racked with tremors, and still sniveling, Abeo had a hard time grabbing hold of the corn.

Nana frowned. "Tears will not help you here. It will only make things worse, so wipe your face, stop your crying, and do what I have shown you to do." She aimed her chin at a stalk of corn. "That one."

Abeo took the corn in her shaky hands and tried her best to imitate Nana's movements, but the result was poor, leaving the stalk bruised and bent.

Nana clucked her tongue. "That," she said pointedly, "will get you whipped."

14

Abeo wept all through her first night at the shrine. Her small hands were bruised from hours of pulling corn and her back ached from the heavy baskets of produce she had been ordered to haul between the fields and the storage hut.

The question of why her father had left her in that place ran circles in her young mind. Try as she might, she could not come up with an answer,

Sometime during the night, Nana's baby woke, crying for his mother's milk. Abeo listened to the suckling sounds and tried to imagine herself in his place. The vision of being held, rocked, and nursed comforted her. She slipped her thumb between her lips and soon fell into a fitful sleep.

Before morning could completely conquer night, the roosters began crowing, drawing the girls from their slumber. Abeo sat up, rubbed the sleep from her eyes, and felt the sadness and fear from the previous day creep over her once again. She'd dreamed that her father had come for her. The dream had been so vivid that she found it hard to believe it wasn't true. The tears returned, yet not one of the girls offered to comfort her. Nana rose from her mat, hitched her son to her hip, and started across the hut to the door.

"Come on, new girl," she called over her shoulder.

Abeo followed Nana and the other girls through the morning mist, down to the river's edge, where they rinsed their mouths, washed their faces, and filled buckets with water.

Back in the hut, Juba once again doled out the *gari* and they ate. The *gari* bubbled up Abeo's throat like lava. She pressed her lips together and forced it back down.

"Do they feed us nothing else?" she squeaked.

Juba licked her fingers. "Sometimes we get pig's tail."

"Not often though," another girl piped.

Abeo stared down at the white paste; the scent alone turned her stomach. She could not imagine a lifetime of eating nothing but *gari*.

During Abeo's first full day in the field, she watched in horror as Duma pounced on a girl who he'd seen slip a kernel of corn into her mouth. The punishment was brutal. He pummeled her face and shoulders with his fists and when she crumpled to the ground, he continued beating, kicking, and stomping until blood seeped from her eyes and mouth. When Duma was done, he simply walked away, leaving her body sprawled out on the dark earth like a broken doll.

There was nothing anyone could do for her, and even if they could, they wouldn't—lest they suffer the same fate. And so they continued to work, stepping over the girl as if she were a twig.

Abeo saw this and her already fragile psyche cracked. After that, the shock set in like August heat, evaporating every bit of moisture Abeo had, even the spit in her mouth.

Finally, dry-eyed and numb, she questioned the girls as to what had brought them to this horrible existence.

"My mother died when I was born, and then while my father was away on a business trip, his second wife, my stepmother, died. Both times I was there."

"My father started looking at me in the same way he used to look at my mother."

"My brothers and I were in a *tro-tro* that drove into a gully and exploded. I made it out alive, but they didn't. My mother was pregnant at the time. The grief caused her to miscarry. It was a boy child."

One heartbreaking story after the next.

If what the old priest said was true, it seemed from the number of girls at the shrine that there was plenty of bad luck in Ukemby.

"And you, new girl, what bad luck befell your family?"

Abeo honestly didn't know. She was a child, and not made privy to complex family matters. Wasik had been suspended for weeks before Abeo noticed he was home more than not. Wasik, of course, had explained it away by saying that he had chosen to work from home for a little while.

Abeo shrugged. "Nothing," she said.

"It's something or else you wouldn't be here," Nana countered. "Or perhaps *you* did something?"

"*Me?*" Abeo thought about it. What could she have done? She was a good girl. Well-behaved, well-mannered, polite. She was an exceptional student and daughter. Her mother had said as much on numerous occasions and her father had agreed. Nevertheless, Abeo scoured her mind to locate the sin she'd committed that had landed her in this hell on earth. She looked down at her palms, down at the sinewy canals that cut through the calloused flesh, and was slowly reminded of a transgression she'd committed in the recent past. She gasped.

"I-I borrowed my aunt's ring."

"You took it."

"You stole it."

The accusations cut like a machete.

"No!" Abeo wailed. "I was just holding it for her until she came back!"

The other girls smirked.

Anxious to flee the spotlight, Abeo shifted the attention to the youngest child in the hut.

"Little one," she called to Juba, "how long have you been here?"

Juba turned to Nana. "How long, Nana, heh?"

Nana pursed her lips. "Uhm, I think a year now. Yes, you came during the last rainy season."

"Aha, one year." Juba raised her index finger into the air, then bent down and drew a long line in the dirt. "One," she echoed, her face beaming with pride. "You see, I still remember my numbers."

Juba was six years old.

15

Ismae stayed with Thema for two days before Wasik came for her, crawling on his knees like a dog. The neighbors watched and whispered. Thema's husband was embarrassed; he placed a firm hand on Wasik's shoulder and begged him to get up.

"Ismae, Ismae . . ." Wasik wailed, until she came to the door.

He wrapped his arms around her calves and cried so hard his tears soaked her bare feet. "Please come home. I cannot live this life without you and Agwe. Please."

As Wasik groveled, Ismae stared down at the bald spot in the center of his head, which seemed to have grown in recent weeks.

"Can you live without Abeo?" she asked in a voice as cool as arctic ice.

"Please come home where we can d-discuss it," he stammered through his tears.

"I want an answer now, Wasik. Right this moment!"

"You are my wife, Ismae, you need to be by my side."

"Go and get *our* daughter and bring her back."

"B-but Ismae," Wasik blubbered, "she is not our daughter, she i—"

Disgusted, Ismae kicked herself free of his grip and retreated back into the safety of Thema and Joseph's home, leaving Wasik on the front steps, beating his head and calling her name.

When the police came, Wasik didn't argue with the officers, he simply apologized for his behavior, climbed into the borrowed car, and drove home.

That night, when the family was fast asleep, the phone began to ring.

A moment later, Thema rushed into Ismae's room and announced in a panicked voice that Grandmother had called to say that Wasik was threatening to kill himself.

Ismae's heart stopped. "Suicide?"

"Joseph is waiting in the car," Thema said.

When they arrived at the house, Wasik was in bed damp with perspiration. When he looked up at Ismae there was not a flicker of recognition. He mumbled nonsense and flailed his arms wildly whenever she came close.

Ismae called for the family doctor, who came and examined Wasik. The doctor prescribed sedatives, bed rest, and cautioned him to cease his excessive drinking. His words to Ismae were blunt and direct: "Can't you see what all of your nonsense is doing to your husband? If you were my wife I'd . . . If he dies, the blood will be on your hands."

And with that, he left.

After ten days, the sun rose in Wasik's eyes. He emerged from his mental breakdown thin and weak. But this time, when he looked at Ismae, he knew who she was and he smiled.

"My love, you've come back to me," he croaked.

Grandmother cautioned Ismae not to speak of the events that had nearly driven him out of his mind, lest he return to the edge of madness. "Next time," she warned, "he may not recover."

Grandmother's words had rattled Ismae, and in that moment she realized with great shame that her fear of losing Wasik outweighed the loss of Abeo.

Ismae went into the bathroom and gazed at herself in the mirror. She never imagined she could become one of those women who pedestaled their men—no matter the error, no matter the consequence. She certainly never imagined herself a woman—a wife no less—who would side with her betrothed ahead of her child. But there she was, doing just that, and it made her sick to her stomach.

She lifted the lid to the toilet, doubled over, and puked.

Ismae supposed her religion had a hand in it. The Bible was clear. Colossians 3:18 stated that wives were to submit themselves to their husbands. Not only that, but on her wedding day her own mother had reminded her—for the hundredth time—that Ismae's place was not ahead of her husband, not beside him, but *behind* him.

Ismae righted herself and smoothed her damp hair back into place. At the sink, she turned on the faucet.

Divorce was not an option. If she wanted to go to heaven after she died, she would have to seek an annulment, and in Ukemby the Catholic Church was not fond of granting annulments. And even if the Church did concede, Ismae would gain her freedom only to lose her status in the community. Divorced women were frowned upon in Ukemban society and divorced women with children were damn near ostracized.

Ismae raised her eyes to the mirror and spoke to her reflection: "I'm caught between being a good wife and a bad mother."

Grandmother, who had been lurking in the doorway, murmured, "Abeo is not your child, so you are not a bad mother. The one who gave her away at birth is the bad mother."

The days rolled into nights and then weeks.

Thema called one afternoon, inquiring as to when Ismae and Wasik would be bringing Abeo back home.

"Soon. As soon as Wasik is well enough to tell me where he took her, we will go and get her," Ismae lied.

"When will that be?" Thema questioned coldly.

Ismae quietly repeated herself: "Soon."

When the school called, asking about Abeo's whereabouts, Ismae said that she had sent her to a boarding school in London. She also told this fib to Abeo's friends and the parents of those friends. She told this invention to everyone and anyone who asked.

It was worse than if Abeo had died. People reminisced about the dead. But in the Kata household, Abeo's name was hardly ever uttered. It was as if she'd never existed.

They went about their lives, each secretly waiting for the good luck to find them again.

A month later, the phone rang with the first piece of positive news they'd had in close to a year—Wasik had been cleared of any wrongdoing and was to report back to work immediately.

A week after that, Ismae found out that she was pregnant. She made the bittersweet announcement at dinner. Grandmother rose from her chair, clapping, stomping her feet, and ululating.

Wasik grabbed Ismae's hands. "See, I told you it was the right thing to do."

And for the first time, Ismae believed that perhaps it was.

16

Abeo had been at the shrine for four months when Serafine dialed Ismae's telephone number and, after a series of clicking sounds, heard the computer-generated message: *"This number has been disconnected . . ."*

Serafine assumed she'd misdialed, so she hung up and tried again. The same recording blared in her ear. She went into her bedroom, retrieved her address book from the nightstand drawer, and flipped through the pages until she came upon her sister's name and number. She *had* dialed correctly. Serafine picked up the phone again and called Thema to find out what was going on.

"Hello?" Thema's voice was wrapped in a blanket of static.

"Thema?"

"Yes. Who is this, please?"

"Serafine."

"The connection is very bad. I'm sorry, who is speaking?"

"Serafine!"

"Serafine? Oh, hello! What a surprise to hear from—"

"Thema, I have been trying to reach Ismae, but the message says the number is disconnected." More static crackled through the silence that fell between the two women. "Thema? Are you there?"

"Yes, I'm here. I wasn't aware that the number was disconnected," she said, hoping the static camouflaged the lie. "I haven't spoken to Ismae for quite some time."

She had, however, spoken to Ismae recently; had, in fact, seen her in person just days earlier at a department store where she'd spied Ismae admiring an expensive dress. Thema had called out to her and Ismae had raised her head, the sunny smile on her lips fading when she saw who it was.

Her first words stumbled clumsily from her mouth, "Thema, h-hello?" before she shifted her gaze toward a rack of elegant head ties.

Thema's eyes had popped with surprise at the baby bump pushing through the blue-and-white wrap skirt Ismae wore. "My goodness, you're expecting?"

Ismae swung the bulk of the large handbag she carried protectively over her midsection. "Yes, I-I am. We wanted to wait before we told anyone. I know I owe you a phone call, but as you can imagine, I've been a bit out of sorts."

"How is the family?"

"They are well," Ismae replied. "Thank you. And yours?"

"Very good."

Ismae finally raised her eyes to meet Thema's excavating gaze, but she quickly discovered that looking directly into her cousin's eyes unraveled her, so instead she stared at the buttons on her blouse.

"And Abeo, how is she doing?" Thema held her breath and waited for Ismae to say that the girl was back home, that it had all been a terrible misunderstanding.

But Ismae didn't say that. In fact, she ignored the

question altogether and answered one that Thema had not asked. "Yes," she said, reaching for a lavender and gold head tie, "I think this one would be a very good choice for the naming ceremony."

Thema had just stood there blinking in disbelief.

When Thema relayed the encounter to her husband later that day, as well as her intention to call Serafine and inform her what Ismae and Wasik had done to Abeo, Joseph calmly fanned his fingers out on the dining room table. "This is not any of your business, Thema. I think it would be wise to stay out of it," he cautioned.

And now here was Serafine on the other end of the telephone bellowing, "Thema? Thema, are you still there?"

"Yes, yes, I am, Serafine. I will go see Ismae this week," she lied, "and call you back, okay?"

Serafine sighed. "Thank you, Thema."

"Okay. Goodbye, Serafine."

"Goodbye, Thema."

17

Ismae had always been the beautiful one, while Serafine was attractive and intelligent. Their uncle, their father's brother, had always doted on Ismae, but when he saw Serafine's potential he suggested to his brother that he send her to America to complete her education. "The opportunities in America would be better for her," he'd said.

And so their parents packed Serafine off to stay with another uncle in Texas, reminding her that she was to obey her uncle and his wife, and also that it was important that she keep her head in her books, her focus on her studies.

Her uncle and aunt had careers, small children, PTA meetings, and cocktail parties. Serafine seemed to be a responsible young lady, so they believed her when she claimed to be at the library or studying with friends; but maybe they wouldn't have been so trusting if they'd witnessed how the adolescent transformed from honor student to quivering mound of jelly whenever she was in the presence of her math teacher, Clark Forester.

Clark Forester was the complexion of iodine, tall, and broad-shouldered; his smoky eyes made grown women swoon—so an innocent, impressionable teenager didn't stand a chance.

Clark Forester was blatant in his advances on Serafine, and he took every opportunity to *accidentally* brush his hand against her breasts. He was fond of standing at her desk, his crotch just inches from her face, his penis twitching behind the zipper of his khakis.

Serafine was in love.

Mr. Forester asked her to stay after class one day. When the other students had gone, he invited her out for coffee. Serafine didn't drink coffee, but she was so flattered that if he'd invited her out to drink a cup of dirt she would have agreed. He claimed that he had a deep interest in Africa—in Ukemby especially—and wondered if she wouldn't mind giving him a quick overview of the country and the culture.

Serafine called her uncle and told him that she was staying at school to finish a project, and would get a ride home with a friend.

Mr. Forester took Serafine to a coffee shop located in the lobby of a motel. They sat across the table from one another, Serafine melting away with each compliment he paid her.

"You're the most beautiful woman I have ever seen," he said as he reached for her hand. "Your skin is so soft, it feels like silk."

Serafine blushed and crossed her legs at the knee, like a grown-up woman. Mr. Forester lit a cigarette and asked if she'd like one. Serafine said no and then yes, and sucked on the filter until she was dizzy.

He took her to room 112, located at the end of a dark corridor. The carpets were tattered and moldy, the room smelled of smoke. He drew the shades, turned on the television, but kept the volume low.

"Lie down until you feel better," he gently ordered.

Serafine stretched her body across the musty bed-spread and closed her eyes. Mr. Forester sat in a chair across the room, smoking and watching her.

"Would you like me to come lie down beside you?"

Serafine said yes.

The first kiss was warm and tender. He held her chin between his thumb and forefinger, just like she'd seen the leading men in the movies do.

When she was naked, he kissed her everywhere until she thought her body would explode. When he entered her, she whimpered and then cried out and then moaned.

Serafine hadn't wanted a child, not at that tender age, and Mr. Forester hadn't wanted one either—he already had three at home with his wife.

"Can you get rid of it?"

"Abort it?"

"Yes."

Serafine couldn't imagine doing such a thing. "I can't do that."

"Well, keep it then. I don't care. I don't know if it's mine or not, and if you implicate me, I'll deny it and you'll be labeled a whore. Is that what you want? Do you want to be called a whore?"

By the time Serafine's uncle and aunt figured out she was pregnant, she was entering her second trimester. Her uncle pressed his lips together in disappointment and his wife cried.

"Who did this to you?" they asked.

Serafine lied, accusing a boy who had moved with his family to another state.

They pulled her out of school, phoned her parents, apologized profusely, and as further consolation offered to keep the child and raise it as their own.

Serafine's mother declined: "No, the child will come back to Ukemby to be raised by her sister and her husband."

Ismae had been married to Wasik for four years at that point, and had been unable to conceive. "God works in the most mysterious of ways!" Serafine's mother exclaimed.

And so it was decided and then it was done.

Serafine had carried Abeo in her womb, pushed her out into the world, and given her a name, but Wasik and Ismae had done all of the rest.

Abeo was theirs.

The seasons changed and Thema still hadn't returned Serafine's phone call. New York City was in the grip of winter and Serafine was standing at her bedroom window staring out at the falling snowflakes when Abeo's voice sounded in her head as clear as cymbals: "*Aunt Serafine!*"

Serafine whirled around, fully expecting Abeo to be standing in the room. Her heart quickened, and right then and there she picked up the phone and dialed Thema's number.

"Have you spoken to my sister?"

Thema hesitated. "They've gone to England. Wasik is on assignment there. A few months, I think. If all goes well, they might be there for a year," she lied.

Silence.

"England? England?" Serafine echoed in disbelief. "I don't understand why they wouldn't tell me. England?"

she repeated slowly. "It's not like them not to say something. Do you have their number in . . . England?"

What was Thema to say? This was not her problem; her husband had made that quite clear.

I had the number, but misplaced it.

Last I heard they were doing quite fine.

I'm sure you will be hearing from them soon.

Serafine placed the phone back on its base, stumbled to the kitchen, and slung open every single cabinet door until she found the bottle of vodka she kept for company.

18

As Serafine poured herself into the bottom of the liquor bottle, Abeo was standing in her hut, poking her bloated stomach with the tip of her pinkie finger. Her swollen abdomen was the direct result of the steady diet of *gari*, which clogged her intestines and made it virtually impossible for her to defecate. When she did—which was rare—there was blood in her stool. Her arms and legs had become as thin as sapling limbs, her vision was weak, and there was a sizable cavity in her back left molar.

Darkwa entered the hut and pointed a cuticle-ravaged finger at Aymee. "You," she said, "golden girl, come with me."

Aymee was so called because of her fair skin and light-colored eyes. She gave the girls a fretful look and then obediently followed Darkwa out the door.

In the field, Abeo whispered to Nana, "Where did she take her?"

Nana pretended not to hear. She tore the husk from the corn and dropped the ear down into the basket.

"Psst, you, Nana. Where did she take Aymee?"

Nana huffed, "To the priest, I suppose. Now stop asking me questions and do your work. All your talking will get us into trouble."

Later they returned to the hut to find Aymee lying on her mat, despondent. She'd gnawed her fleshy bottom lip raw.

Nana shook her shoulder. "Aymee, Aymee," she coaxed as she stared into the girl's glassy eyes. "Give me a wet cloth," Nana said to no one in particular.

Juba unwrapped the cloth from her head, dunked it into a bucket of water, and handed it to her.

Nana gently mopped the dried blood from Aymee's chin. As Abeo watched, her hand floated to her own lip.

Juba hovered nervously. She opened and closed her mouth a number of times before finally asking, "What's wrong with her? Is she ill?"

Nana continued to tend to Aymee in silence. She handed the bloody cloth back to Juba, then leaned back on her haunches.

Juba pressed, "Is Aymee ill?"

Nana shook her head in the solemn way Abeo had seen elders do during the most grave moments. "Aymee is not ill. She has been touched by the hand of God."

After the hand of God touched Aymee, she was next touched by Duma. She returned wrapped in a blanket of sadness that spread among the girls like a virus.

Abeo and Juba did not know what was being done and no one would tell them. But Abeo knew that it had to be a very bad thing, because three days later Darkwa came for another girl named Kenya, and when she returned to the hut, she was batting at her ears and muttering like a madwoman. "He put it in me! He put it in me!"

When Nana couldn't take any more, she threw a bucket of water at her and Kenya fell silent.

Abeo was thankful for the quiet, but couldn't help wondering exactly what the priest had put in Kenya.

Later that same night, Nana's moaning pulled them from their sleep.

"It's coming," Nana groaned.

Abeo sat up. "What's coming?" She rubbed her eyes and stared at the shadowy silhouettes that scurried through the darkness.

Nana was sitting against the wall, head thrown back, knees aimed at the straw-thatched ceiling.

Abeo jumped from her mat. "What's happening?"

"The baby's coming!" Juba exclaimed.

"She must go to hospital then!" Abeo screeched.

One of the other girls ran out of the hut and returned with two elder *trokosi*. They rushed into the hut carrying kerosene lamps.

Nana hollered in pain.

One of the elder *trokosi* ordered, "Bring water!"

Abeo and Kenya watched, frozen.

"Push!" the women commanded, pinning her flailing arms.

Nana growled that she couldn't, that she wouldn't push.

They told her she would and she could. "You must!"

Nana screamed, and this time Abeo screamed along with her.

"Ah, yes, I see the head," one woman said. "Push again!"

Abeo held her breath, clenched her empty womb, and bore down for Nana.

"Push!"

Nana howled like a wounded antelope and the baby burst out with an ocean of blood.

Abeo's jaw dropped.

One woman covered the baby's mouth with her own, sucked, and then spat the gunk onto the ground. She did the same to its nose and then opened its legs to see the sex. Satisfied, she nodded and handed the baby off to the other woman.

"It's a boy," she announced. "The gods will be pleased."

19

As Nana recovered from giving birth, Ismae grappled with nausea and stomach cramps. She had not felt well for most of the morning and had refused breakfast. A trip to the bathroom revealed spots of blood in the seat of her underwear, sending her into a panic.

"Just go lie down and elevate your feet," Grandmother advised.

Ismae followed the old woman's instructions and soon she was fast asleep. When Wasik returned home from work, he walked into the bedroom to find Ismae unresponsive in a pool of blood.

At the hospital, Dr. Lomi brought Wasik to a quiet room. "I'm afraid she's lost a lot of blood and has fallen into a coma."

"When w-will she come out of the coma?" Wasik asked.

The doctor gave him a sober look. "You cannot put a time on these things. It is in God's hands now," he mumbled. He left Wasik gazing down at his shoes like a lost little boy, wondering *which* god his wife's fate had been left to.

Hours later, a nurse who happened to be a childhood

friend of both Thema and Ismae called Thema with the sad news.

In the hospital, Thema could do little else but sit at Ismae's bedside and cry. When Wasik walked in, ruffled and dazed, it took everything in her not to spit in his face. But she refrained because there was blood on her hands too. She'd told Serafine an elaborate lie, and maybe if she'd told the truth, Ismae wouldn't be in this hospital fighting for her life. Yes, she had blood all over her hands.

And who knew what Wasik was prepared to do to save Ismae? He might take Agwe to a shrine—Thema knew some of the shrines took little boys.

The truth had to be told. So Thema went to the pay phone and called Serafine collect.

"Hello?"

"Serafine, it's Thema. I need you to listen very carefully to what I'm about to say."

20

"You're getting fat," Juba said to Aymee when she handed her the bowl of *gari*.

Aymee looked down at herself. It was true. She was gaining weight. Her breasts had ballooned in size and her waist was thick.

"Maybe you're eating too much *gari*, heh?" Juba joked. They all laughed.

"Perhaps," Juba ventured, pointing at the door, "you are eating the corn when no one is watching?"

"Or," Nana added, as she lifted her infant son to her shoulder, "you will be having one of *these* in a few months."

Abeo realized that she was now the only one laughing and clamped her mouth shut.

Aymee frowned. "No, no," she whispered, briskly shaking her head.

"Ah," Nana moaned, gently patting the baby's back, "you cannot be that stupid, can you?"

Aymee just stared at her.

Nana pointed at the girl's stomach. "It's not *gari* that's making you fat, it's *baby* that's making you fat."

"No, that cannot be," Aymee whined, wide-eyed. She tried to back away from her swollen midsection, but it followed.

"Well, believe what you want," Nana spat. "In a few months' time you will know the truth."

Aymee began to cry, sending Abeo into a rage: "Why are you saying these things?"

Nana shrugged her shoulders. "Because they are true."

"They are *not* true!" Abeo screeched, and hurled her bowl of *gari* across the room. "You are a liar. You are just saying these things to be mean!"

Nana's eyes moved to the bowl and then back to Abeo. "We don't have to talk about it anymore. Time will tell who is the liar and who is not, and then you will remember this day." She pointed to the bowl. "Now, clean up that mess before we're invaded by ants."

Several weeks later, Nana was moved to another hut with three girls who also had children.

With each day, Aymee grew wider. She complained that her legs felt as heavy as tree trunks. She had a hard time keeping down the *gari*, and in the fields the sun made her sleepy and sluggish, so she could not pick her weight in corn. Abeo covered for her by picking enough for the both of them.

When they went to the river to bathe, Abeo noticed that the area around Aymee's nipples was very dark and that the nipples themselves were thick and elongated. Abeo recalled the changes her mother's body had undergone when she was pregnant with Agwe, and suddenly realized that what Nana had said about Aymee was true.

Toward the end of the harvesting season, the clouds gathered and it stormed for three straight days.

Juba and Abeo stood at the open door gazing at the deluge.

"I will be seven years old very soon, I think," Juba offered whimsically. She looked at Abeo. "Have you ever had a birthday party?"

"Ah-huh," Abeo replied.

"I had one when I was three, or maybe I was four. I forget," Juba said. "I am forgetting a lot of things."

Abeo pushed her hand out into the rain.

"It was nice, really, really nice. There were balloons and cake."

"You remember so far back? Three or four?" Kenya questioned from behind them.

Juba spun around. "Yes, I do. And I remember I had a cake as big as this hut . . ."

"As big as this hut? Really?" Aymee laughed.

"Well, maybe not that big. But it was very, very big. As big as . . ." Juba's eyes wandered wildly. "Ah!" she cried, pointing to her mat. "It was as big as that!"

Abeo smiled. "Yes, yes, that was a very big cake. You must have been a very, very good girl."

Juba beamed. "I was. I was very good. And smart! I did very well in school."

"No ruler for you?" Aymee teased, slapping her fingers across her knuckles.

"Not for me!" Juba exclaimed. "That ruler was for the wicked children, not Juba!"

They all bubbled with laughter.

"Stop it," Aymee cried. "You are going to make me wet myself!"

For the moment they sounded like happy, well-fed, well-loved children. It wasn't as if laughter never rang at the shrine. The smaller children laughed all the time. But that joy disappeared when they reached the age of six and were forced to exchange their bliss for hard labor.

Finally, Abeo's laughter dwindled to giggles and hiccups. By the time Aymee and Juba were able to get their own crowing under control, Abeo had moved out of the hut and into the rain. She raised one foot and then the next until she was dancing in the muddy puddles. Soon, she was whirling like a top. Spinning so fast that the rain flew from her body in sheets. Abeo closed her eyes and chanted the words from her favorite movie: *"There's no place like home, there's no place like home . . ."*

"Hey you!"

The blow to her gut sent her stumbling. She tripped over her wet feet and fell down with a splat while the world continued to loop. When she blinked the water from her eyes, Duma swam into view. The brim of the canvas hat he wore was weighted with water. The spillage cascaded over his face like a wet curtain.

Abeo coughed and sprayed *gari* and blood-tainted saliva into the downpour.

"Get inside! You'll get a fever out here in the rain. And then how will you work?" Duma shouted.

The girls watched quietly from the doorway as Abeo hurried toward them. Thunder boomed across the sky and Abeo imagined that the gods were laughing at her.

21

The ten-hour flight from New York to Ukemby, her passage through immigration and then customs, the time she spent waiting for her luggage to appear on the carousel—all of this happened in a fog. Reality didn't take hold of Serafine until she exited Toko International Airport and stepped into the blistering-hot chaos of Port Masi.

Men swarmed from all directions. "Carry your bag, miss? Carry your bag?"

Serafine waved them away, then stuck a Marlboro between her chapped lips and lit it.

People stared. It was unusual to see a woman smoking in public. Serafine ignored the attention, smoked the cigarette down to the butt, dropped it to the ground, and mashed it beneath the sole of her Italian leather pump.

In the taxi, the driver spoke to her reflection in the rearview mirror: "Sister, you live in America a long time, huh?"

Serafine ignored his question and repeated her destination: "Filster Hospital."

She hated hospitals. Hated the smell of them. The sick and dying all reeked the same no matter their race or religion. Serafine paced the corridor outside of Ismae's room until she could summon the nerve to enter. She was conscious of the sound of her heels against the linoleum floor and the beeping of the machinery keeping Ismae alive. Those sounds, combined with the drumroll of her heart, unnerved her.

Serafine gazed down into Ismae's serene face. She looked dead. Fighting back tears, Serafine lowered herself into the chair next to the bed and took her sister's limp, warm hand in her own.

"You're just resting, that's all; and soon you'll wake up and be as good as new," she proclaimed aloud.

Serafine filled her time with Ismae with loving tasks: she combed her hair, clipped her fingernails, and ran ice chips over her parched lips. She hummed as she worked; sometimes she spoke in low tones, reminiscing about their childhood. She hoped and prayed that Ismae could hear her from way down in that black hole she'd slipped into.

After some time, jet lag plummeted down on her. "I'll come back tomorrow morning," she promised as she gathered her things. She leaned over and planted a soft kiss on Ismae's forehead. "I love you."

When the taxi came to a halt in front of her sister's home, Serafine was surprised to see that the place still looked the same. She'd half expected the house to be covered in vines with a family of crows perched on the rooftop.

She took a deep breath, climbed the steps, set her bag down, and knocked on the door. Grandmother opened it with Agwe in her arms.

"Wasik didn't tell me you were coming."

"He didn't know."

She waited for the old woman to move out of the way; when she didn't, Serafine stepped around her and rolled her suitcase into the house. She stopped briefly at the closed door of Abeo's room before continuing on to the guest bedroom. Grandmother followed close behind.

"How long will you be staying?"

"Until I find Abeo," Serafine huffed, and then quietly closed the door in the old woman's face.

22

At the shrine, Aymee gave birth to a copper-colored boy, who she named Ofi. Abeo and the rest of the girls fussed over him like he was their very own.

Two days after Ofi was born, Juba walked into the hut, closed the door, and pressed her back against the wall. The muscles in her face were tense; sweat covered her brown forehead and trickled down her temples.

"Are you okay?" Abeo asked, sidling up to her.

Juba gave her a cryptic look. "Shhh."

Aymee plucked her nipple from Ofi's mouth. "What's wrong," she whispered.

Juba parted her feet, and a mango plopped down to the ground. "A gift for you and Ofi," she breathed.

They all stared at the mango as if it were a brick of gold.

"You stole it?"

Juba grinned. "It fell off the truck and rolled to the side of the road. I didn't steal it, I rescued it!"

The girls exchanged fearful looks.

"You should have left it there," Kenya warned.

All of their eyes bounced nervously between the door and the mango.

Aymee hissed, "They'll beat you if they find out."

Abeo put her finger to her lips and the girls went silent. A shadow had appeared beneath the door. In a flash, Juba kicked the mango across the hut; Aymee swiped it up and hid it behind her back just as the door swung open.

Duma swaggered in. "What's going on in here?" He posed the question to Juba, who lowered her eyes and shook her head. "Heh?" He looked at Abeo.

"Nothing," she mumbled.

"*Nothing?*" he mocked, then strolled over to Aymee and peered down at Ofi. "I make pretty, pretty babies, don't you think?" He reached down and stroked Aymee's collarbone. "I said I make pretty babies."

"Y-yes," Aymee responded.

"Ha!" Duma clapped his hands and spun around. He approached Abeo and caught her by the chin. "Maybe one day, you and I will make pretty babies together?"

Abeo gulped and shifted her eyes to the window.

Duma chuckled, turned around, swept his gaze around the hut, and left without another word. When they were sure he was gone, Aymee produced the mango from behind her back, pressed it lovingly against her cheek, brought it to her nose, and inhaled.

"Hurry," Juba urged.

Aymee quickly peeled the skin and took a bite. She closed her eyes and savored the sweetness. She had not had a mango in months. "Here," she said, pushing the fruit toward Juba.

"No, it's for you," Juba said.

"Take a bite. All of you must have some," Aymee insisted.

Juba took a small nibble.

"Come on, Juba, a little more," Aymee pressed.

This time Juba sunk her teeth in and pulled off a thick wad of the sweet stringy flesh. Eyes twinkling, she moaned, "It's so good."

She passed the mango to Abeo, who took a bite and then passed it on to Kenya.

"Tomorrow, maybe I will rescue an orange," Juba laughed.

The next day, Juba rescued two bananas, which the girls mashed and mixed in with the *gari*—it was a meal fit for queens.

23

Wasik pulled the car into the driveway, turned off the headlights, and just sat there, savoring the silence. He'd called the house and Grandmother told him that Serafine was there, so he knew he would be walking into a fury.

He lowered all of the car windows and the quiet night seeped in. He was scrutinizing his tired face in the rearview mirror when the darkness in the backseat shifted. Wasik lurched around in surprise, but there was nothing there, save for a black umbrella and a day-old newspaper.

Inside the house the phone rang twice and then Serafine's chilling screams hacked away at the hush like a rusted saber.

Abeo had dreamed that her belly swelled as big as the sun. In the dream she peeled away her brown flesh to reveal a smiling, pink-gummed baby.

The dream remained with her all through the day, and that evening, as Wasik stumbled from his car, she pondered it further while she sat eating her *gari*.

"What are you thinking about?" Aymee asked.

"I had a very strange dream last night. I dreamed I was pregnant."

Aymee's eyebrows climbed. "Pregnant?"

"Yes."

"Hmmm, my grandmother used to say when one dreams of pregnancy, it means the opposite," Kenya said.

"The opposite?" Juba's voice oozed with curiosity as she juggled the day's "rescued" oranges.

"Yes, I have heard the same thing," Aymee offered quietly.

"Dreaming of death means that someone is about to bring life into the world. Dreaming of a new life means that a life will soon be removed from the world."

Juba tossed one of the oranges to Aymee, who caught it and plunged her thumb deep into the navel, splitting it clean down to the center.

Suddenly, Duma kicked the door open and charged into the hut like a wild boar. Aymee shoved the fruit beneath the belly of her sleeping child, but the evidence of its presence hung in the air like expensive perfume.

Duma stood with his hands on his hips, snorting like the animal he was. "A-ha!" he cackled, wagging his finger at the terrified girls, "give it to me, you little thieves!"

Aymee hurriedly removed the squashed fruit from beneath the baby and held it out to him. He glared at her. "You like oranges, heh?"

Aymee lowered her eyes. Duma snatched the fruit from her shaking hands, crushed it in his fist, and then smashed it into her face.

"Get up!" he yelled. Aymee rose obediently to her feet. "Outside!" He pointed to the door.

"No!" Juba screamed. "I took it, not her."

Duma's eyes narrowed. "Really? You, little Juba, a thief?"

Juba swallowed, nodded her head. "I . . . it rolled from the truck—"

"Did it now?"

"Yes."

He took a step closer to her. "You are lying, aren't you?"

Juba looked at Aymee. "Yes, I am. I took it from the basket."

"You stole it. Say you *stole* it."

"I stole it from the basket."

"Then you must be punished. Stealing from the gods is a serious offense."

Juba nodded in agreement, raised her head high into the air, peered directly into Duma's eyes, and announced, "Yes, I must be punished."

Juba followed Duma to a cluster of neem trees and he bound her to the one with the trunk shaped like a crooked walking stick. There, he poured cane juice over her body and left her to the red ants.

The ants covered Juba like a blanket, stinging every inch of her body until she begged for mercy. In the hut, Abeo and the rest of the girls huddled together in a trembling mass with their hands clamped over their ears.

Three hours. One hundred and eighty minutes. Juba screamed until she was hoarse. Only then did Duma untie her.

At the river, Abeo and Kenya washed the cane juice from the girl's body, taking tender care around her bloated lips and swollen eyes. The poor thing was covered from head to toe in angry red blotches.

That night as they lay on their separate mats, each lost in her own thoughts, Juba whispered into the darkness, "Abeo, do you think your dream was about me?"

Abeo rolled onto her side to face her. In the scant moonlight, Juba looked like a wounded angel. "No, no, Juba. It was not about you."

"How can you be sure?"

Abeo sighed. "Why would you think such a thing?"

"Because sometimes I pray to die."

24

Wasik sat before Ismae's closed coffin with Agwe squirming in his lap. All of the mourners were gone; just Serafine and the priest remained. Grandmother had returned to the air-conditioned limousine.

Serafine and the priest stood waiting beneath the sparse shade of a baobab tree as Wasik said his final farewells. The sun shifted west and a gust blew in from the north, setting the limbs of a nearby sausage tree to trembling.

Serafine lit a cigarette and inhaled. When she blew the smoke out of the side of her mouth, she caught the eyes of the old priest glaring at her disapprovingly.

"Sorry," she muttered, and dropped the cigarette to the ground. The priest pulled a tissue from his pocket, bent down, and retrieved the butt. "S-sorry," Serafine muttered again before hooking the straps of her pocketbook over her shoulder. "Come on, Wasik, let's go."

Wasik could barely walk. He leaned on the priest for support, and kept turning around to look at the coffin, hoping against hope that this was someone else's funeral, praying to the gods that Ismae would leap out from behind one of the trees flashing that beautiful smile he loved so much.

As deep as Wasik's sorrow was, Serafine was suffering twofold. She had lost her sister and her daughter. She knew she couldn't raise Ismae from the dead, but she had hope that she would still find Abeo.

So, back at the house when Wasik filled his tumbler with schnapps and went out to the veranda, Serafine followed.

"I'm going to ask you again, Wasik: where did you take Abeo?"

In the darkness, Wasik looked as small as a child. When he turned to face her, his eyes were soupy with grief. "Huh?"

"Where did you take Abeo?" Serafine grabbed his hands and squeezed. "Please, Wasik, tell me," she pleaded, on the verge of tears.

"You see that star?" he said, pointing at the sky. "That's the North Star. It seems brighter tonight, don't you think?"

"Wasik? Wasik, please," Serafine sobbed. "Abeo. I need you to tell me where you took her."

Wasik smiled. It was a sad smile, but a smile just the same. "I-I think . . ." he began in a slow, childlike voice, "I think that's Ismae's way of telling me that she is okay. That we're all going to be okay."

"Wasik, please!" Serafine shrilled.

He drained the glass. "No, Serafine, I cannot tell you that."

"But why?"

"Because," Wasik sniffed, "I do not remember."

And he didn't. His memory before the night Ismae died was blank. He could barely recall the last seven days.

Serafine pressed her fingers against her temples. "What do you mean you don't remember?"

Wasik rolled the glass tumbler nervously between his palms. "I just don't remember," he echoed flatly.

Serafine exploded. She grabbed Wasik by his collar and slapped him twice across of the face. He didn't make an effort to defend himself, he just stood there silently, swaying like a reed.

She decided that if she could not make him talk, then maybe the police could.

"My daughter is missing," she told the officer who took the call.

"How long?"

"I don't know, months!"

The police came an hour later. Serafine babbled on like a madwoman, swinging an accusatory finger between Grandmother and Wasik. The officers listened, but every time Serafine mentioned *trokosi* or the shrine, they took a measured step away from her.

The officers looked at Wasik, who sat mute, staring blankly at a potted plant. Grandmother, who had said nothing while Serafine raged, finally spoke, and the tale she told was littered with lies.

"No child has been taken, but a life has been lost. Just today my son buried his wife, who was also her sister," she pointed at Serafine, "and now they are both wild with grief."

The police officers' jurisdiction did not cover the spiritual realm, and besides, *trokosi* may have been considered immoral by some, but it wasn't illegal, and so they bid the family good night and left.

Serafine called Thema. "Come and get me, I can't stay here."

Away from Wasik and his mother, Serafine cried into Thema's shoulder until she had no more tears, and then she asked, "Will you and Joseph take me to the shrine?"

Thema folded her hands in her lap. "There are many shrines, Serafine."

"Many?" Serafine blinked. "Do you mean ten or twenty?" Her voice dripped with hope. They could easily do ten or twenty—they could do that in a matter of days.

Thema exchanged a look with her husband and then whispered, "There are hundreds, maybe thousands."

Serafine's heart sank. "How can that be?"

"It just is," Joseph sighed.

The next day, the three headed out early in the morning. Joseph did not have any faith in their expedition, but Serafine had paced the house all night long, mumbling and crying. What could he do, ignore her? After all, he was a parent too.

They drove in silence. Thema sat in the front seat gnawing on her thumbnail and staring out the window. Serafine sat in the back, her eyes wide and watching.

"How much farther?" Serafine asked repeatedly.

Joseph felt the hair on his neck begin to rise. It wasn't like those places were listed on a map. Fetish priests did not advertise the location of their shrines. Either you knew where one was or you knew someone who knew someone who could tell you. And Joseph knew someone. "I think it's just up the road here on the left," he said.

He drove the car into the shrine and a group of small children magically appeared, buzzing with excitement as they swarmed toward the car.

A tall, thin boy shooed them away, planted himself in the path of the vehicle, and raised his hand for Joseph to stop. A second later, four men appeared and surrounded the car like soldiers.

Serafine vaulted out and rushed toward the cluster of children. She anxiously scanned each and every one of their faces. "Do you know Abeo? Abeo Kata. Do you know her?"

The children sang back, "What did you bring for us, mama? Candy?"

The slim boy lunged at her, but Serafine skirted quickly from his reach, running aimlessly, hysterically screaming Abeo's name.

Joseph jumped from the car and started after the boy who was quickly gaining on Serafine. He caught the kid by the wrist and he whirled around in surprise, his free hand poised to strike. Joseph threw his own hands up in surrender. "I will contain her," Joseph assured him, and took off behind Serafine.

Thema, terrified, locked the doors and watched the absurd scene from the safety of the car.

Joseph cornered Serafine between a tree and a hut. "Serafine!" he panted. "This is not the way. We must go see the priest."

The priest was on the far side of the shrine, unaware of the pandemonium Serafine had caused. He sat napping beneath a massive silk cotton tree and was stirred awake when the trio approached.

The boy whispered into the old man's ear. The priest shot Joseph a curious look before nodding for him to state his reason for being there.

"Father," Joseph said, "I have come to see if my niece is here."

The old man studied him with jaundiced eyes. "Her name?"

"Abeo Kata!" Serafine shrieked from behind Joseph.

The priest cocked his head to one side and smiled at Serafine. "The women in Port Masi have forgotten their place. Their tongues are loose." He shifted his gaze to Joseph. "You need to learn how to control your wife."

"She is not my wife," Joseph said. "She is the mother of the child I seek."

The priest coughed, used the back of his hand to wipe the spittle from his lips, and said, "There is no Abeo Kata here."

Two weeks and four shrines later, Joseph and Thema drove Serafine back to the airport.

"There must be hundreds of shrines," Thema had murmured after the third disappointment. "Maybe even thousands," she said, repeating what she had told Serafine from the start.

Their mission was hopeless.

25

Abeo had been thinking a lot about slaves. Sometimes she dreamed that she was in the stinking dungeons of Elmina Castle, running through its dark tunnels and corridors, until she finally burst through the Door of No Return and dove into the ocean where she transformed into a whale the color of a rainbow. When she woke from those dreams, her lips always tasted of salt.

All she had now were her dreams. The memories of her former life had slowly evaporated; the faces of her family and friends were now faded like the images in old photographs. Abeo had even begun to question her very existence. There were days where she doubted that she had even been born, convinced that she had always been in this place, having sprung from the soil like the corn she harvested.

The day Abeo's life changed again, she and the other girls were bathing in the river.

"Did you cut yourself?" Juba asked.

Abeo shook her head, rinsed her hand in the rushing water, and then swiped it between her legs. Another red smear.

Kenya waded over. "Let me see." After looking at

Abeo's hand, her eyes wandered fearfully to Duma, who was sitting in his usual spot on the hill, tossing peanuts into his mouth. She took Abeo by the hand and led her toward the riverbank and back to the hut.

"Am I sick?" Abeo asked, her voice dripping with fear.

In the hut Kenya handed her a cloth. "Put that between your legs. Is this your first time?"

"First time for what?"

Kenya pointed at her crotch. "Is this the first time you are seeing the blood?"

Abeo nodded.

"It is your cycle. You will bleed every month now. It's what happens when you become a woman."

Abeo didn't understand; she was just eleven years old. "I am not a woman."

"Yes, today you have become a woman. Here," Kenya placed the cloth in Abeo's hand, "put it between your legs. You're making a mess."

Abeo looked down to see droplets of blood seeping into the dirt.

Kenya moved closer and whispered, "If Duma knows about this he will tell, and Darkwa will come for you after your third cycle."

"Come for me? Come for me for what?"

"To bring you to the priest."

Abeo frowned.

Kenya continued: "And he will touch you with the hand of God and your belly will grow big with child."

Abeo began to tremble. "Don't say that!" She balled her fists and charged at Kenya, but Aymee caught her by her wrist before she could land the first punch.

"Stop it, Abeo!" Aymee scolded. "Kenya is only tell-ing you the truth."

Kenya said, "Abeo, we don't know if Duma saw. If he didn't, we can keep you safe."

Abeo raised her head; her cheeks shimmered with tears. "Can you keep me safe forever?"

"No," Kenya responded unhappily, "we cannot."

As it turned out, they would not even be able to keep it from Duma for one day, because he'd seen the blood on Abeo's hand—he had the eyes of an eagle—and had brought the news to his father. By then, however, the priest was old.

Duma was a mirror of what the priest had been de-cades earlier—as fierce as a lion and wholly devoted to the practice of *trokosi*—so when Duma reported that the girl called Abeo had seen her first menstrual cycle, the priest gave him permission to act as the human conse-crator that would seal Abeo to Yame forever.

In that place, months passed with the sluggishness of years. After the second month, the urgency surround-ing the blood was forgotten—the girls thought they had outsmarted Duma.

At night they boasted: "He is so stupid!" They laughed, forgetting that The Evil One was like a god, and also possessed the ability to see and hear all.

Two weeks after Abeo completed her third menstrual cycle, Darkwa darkened the doorway of their hut and pointed at Abeo. "You, come with me."

She took Abeo to the ritual bathing hut located at the far end of the shrine. Waiting inside were three el-der *trokosi*.

"Take off your dress, remove your beads."

Abeo did so without question.

In the center of the room was a large barrel filled with water.

"Get in."

The water was warm and aromatic. All four women washed her, each concentrating on one section of her body. They chanted as they worked.

When they were done they mashed chunks of shea butter between their palms and slathered it onto her damp body, working it deep into her skin, until she shone like a freshly buffed shoe.

It was dark outside when they slipped the white robe over Abeo's head and delivered her to Duma.

She had a sense of what was to follow. Muted like a foghorn, Kenya's words resounded in her ear: *He put it in me!* Aymee's words followed: *He will touch you with the hand of God and your belly will grow big with child.*

It was 1987 and Abeo was eleven years, six months, and twenty-two days old.

26

A decade after Duma took Abeo's virginity, he followed his father into the mango groves with a copy of the *Freedom Journal* clutched in his hand. The old priest moved slowly between the rows, stopping every so often to examine the fruit that hung heavy from the stems. Three of his wives trailed a safe distance behind them, ready to jump at his beck and call.

"Father, I need to speak with you," Duma pressed.

The priest did not acknowledge his son's request, but continued to hobble forward until he reached the edge of the grove. "Help me," he demanded when they came upon the cool shade of a plantain tree. Duma guided the old man down to the ground. There, he surveyed the lush countryside, and a look of deep satisfaction settled on his face.

Duma waited a few moments before diving in: "Father, please, I have important news."

The priest pulled a plump mango from the pocket of his robe and worked feverishly at removing the skin. "Speak," he mumbled.

Duma unrolled the newspaper and read. But because his formal education had ended when he was eleven years old, the sentences tumbled awkwardly from his mouth. He labored over the pronunciation of the words, stopping often to slowly retrace sentences. When he reached the end of the article, the priest looked at him and asked, "What does it all mean?"

Duma folded the newspaper and looked directly into his father's milky eyes. "It means the government has outlawed what we do here. It means no more *trokosi*."

The priest clucked his tongue and laughed. He raised the mango to his mouth and sunk his brittle teeth into it. He chewed the flesh slowly and thoughtfully.

"Father?"

The priest swiped the back of his hand across his lips, gazed down at the partially eaten mango, and chuckled. "My son, why are you so worried?"

Duma's eyes bulged. "Have you not heard anything I've read?" He shook the paper at his father.

"Yes, yes, I heard every word."

"And?"

"Help me up."

When the priest was on his feet again, he planted his hands firmly on Duma's shoulders. "Listen, my son, there is nothing to be concerned about. No man's law can change the commandments that have been put in place by the gods." He gave his son a squeeze. "The Ukemban government has no jurisdiction here." And with that, he turned and started the long trek back through the groves.

Duma was so relieved, he tore the newspaper into long shreds and tossed them high into the air.

Abeo was working in a nearby field when one of the girls spotted the swirling papers and nudged her. "Look," she cried happily, "butterflies!"

Abeo glanced up and for one fleeting moment her spirit soared. Indeed, at that distance, the bits of newspaper did appear to be a cluster of white butterflies. Abeo watched until the air went still and the false butterflies dropped out of sight.

It was 1998 and Abeo was twenty-two years, eight months, and seventeen days old.

After that first time with Duma, Abeo had made an attempt to escape. One dark night, she shook Juba and the other girls awake.

"I'm leaving here."

"To go where?"

"Home."

"Home? Your family doesn't want you. Our families don't want any of us."

"I don't believe that," Abeo whispered. "Come with me."

"No, no, we can't," Juba cried. "We'll be caught, or worse, killed by wild animals."

"I'd rather be dead than here," Abeo scoffed.

She stole out into the black night. Her heart roared in her ears as she streaked into the cornfields. There was no moon that night, so Abeo was forced to move blindly through the rows of corn. She felt something brush against her cheek, cried out, and took off in the opposite direction. She thought she heard feet pounding behind her, and dropped to the ground, pressing herself against the dry earth.

Finally, confident that she wasn't being pursued, Abeo rose to her feet and carefully trekked her way through the darkness.

She had no idea that she was moving in circles.

Weary, but thinking she had traveled a great distance from the shrine, Abeo laid down to rest and in a moment was fast asleep. When she opened her eyes, it was morning and Duma was looming over her with his belt coiled around his fist. He used the buckle end to whip Abeo all the way back to her hut.

By the time the government placed a ban on ritual servitude, Kenya had birthed two children and Nana was blind. The rumor that circulated among the *trokosi* was that Duma had flown into a rage, plucked out her eyes, and consumed them with his evening meal. Nana's disability prevented her from working in the fields, so every day at dawn she was driven into town, given a bowl, and left to sit, begging for change beneath a neem tree.

Juba was long dead. When her time had arrived, she'd fought like a wildcat—kicking Duma between his legs before fleeing to the river. There, Duma tackled her to the ground and stunned her with one hard blow to her nose. He mounted her right there on the wet soil. When Duma was done, he left her sprawled on the riverbank gazing at the stars.

Juba eventually sat up, announced to the rising sun that she was eleven years old, and drew two long lines in the dirt. "Eleven," she whispered. "See, I still remember my numbers."

After that, she walked over to a golden shower tree dripping with yellow blooms. She climbed up into the branches, removed her robe, and fashioned it into a noose.

Juba's dead body stayed hidden for days behind the

veil of lush green leaves and broad yellow petals, and might have remained concealed forever if not for the buzzards.

27

At one hundred and four years, the old priest finally died, leaving his eldest son as his successor. Under Duma's rule, the shrine became a brothel, with men from the surrounding villages paying Duma to have sex with the girls.

Those men would slither into the huts, drunk with beer, calling through the darkness, "Sweet girl, sweet girl . . ."

They'd force their fingers into the young mouths. "Start with this," they'd murmur, "and work your way down."

Sometimes fathers brought their sons—schoolboys who barely understood the workings of their own bodies, never mind that of a woman's.

They were all the same to Abeo: fathers, sons, old men, young boys, Duma—all deplorable, all despicable.

So no, Abeo didn't know who had fathered her son, a son who looked a lot like her baby brother—but the not-knowing didn't make her love the child any less.

With baby Pra secured safely to her back, Abeo hoisted the basket filled with roasted corn into the cab of the truck and climbed in. The vehicle belched smoke as it rumbled down the narrow rutted road that emptied into a wider artery pocked with craters.

Their destination was the busy town of Aboão, which sat on the border between Ukemby and Togo. The streets of Aboão bustled with travelers, most of whom were young white foreigners armed with Bradt travel guides, strapped with colorful backpacks. Money hawkers stood on every corner bellowing the exchange rates for the day. They were often drowned out by the noise of the vans that inched through the streets blaring funeral announcements from loudspeakers.

With the baskets atop their heads, the girls joined the bedlam of street hawkers. They moved fluidly between the automobiles. Ambivalent to the blistering sun, the burn of exhaust smoke against their calves, and the watching eyes of their overseers. They shouted out the day's prices:

"One cendi!"

"Fifty pese!"

"Two cendi!"

"Eighty-five pese!"

Money and product exchanged hands until the baskets were empty.

Taylor Adams sat at a roadside café sipping a Coke. Her eyes ping-ponged between the girls and the men who watched them.

"Penny for your thoughts?" said her friend Allen.

Taylor barely glanced at his nutmeg-colored face. A wisp of a smile bloomed and died on her lips.

Allen followed her eyes with his own. "Yes, I know."

"It's disgusting," she spat. "They haven't had a drink of water in . . ." she looked down at her wristwatch, "at all!"

Allen eyed the glass jug of water on the table between them.

"It's ninety degrees in the blasted shade, for goodness sakes," Taylor continued angrily.

Taylor had first traveled to Ukemby in 1994 with
her then-boyfriend and his church and had become instantly smitten with the people and the culture. It was
during that trip that she first learned of the practice of
ritual servitude in Ukemby. These innocent children, almost always female, were known by a variety of names,
but the most common term was *trokosi*. As far as Taylor
was concerned, this practice was just slavery by another
name.

During that trip, Taylor had attended a church ser-
vice where the minister spoke passionately against the
practice. He and his family had taken into their home
a young woman who had been *trokosi* but had fled the
shrine to live in the streets, begging for food. Taylor had
listened with tears in her eyes as the young girl, Abenda,
shared her story with the congregation.

"I was taken to the shrine at the age of five. While
there, I was fed little food and was forced to work in the
fields twelve hours a day. When I stole food, I was beaten
with a stick. I had my first child at the age of eleven, my
second at thirteen. I ran away even though I was told
that if I did so, my family would die. I ran away to my
family and my mother and father shunned me. They said
I had brought shame on them. They threw stones at me
and ordered me to go back to the shrine, but I refused. I
preferred to live in the street like a dog than go back to
that hell."

Taylor returned to New York a changed woman. The

plight of the *trokosi* hovered over her like a rain cloud. She could not get Abenda's story out of her mind.

She tried to research the practice but found that there was little information available. This frustrated and angered Taylor, so she began to send letters to major newspapers and television stations. *Won't someone please do a story about this?* she wrote.

But no one responded. Apparently, little black girls being enslaved, raped, and tortured a continent away wasn't newsworthy.

Taylor Adams was the only child of a black mother and a white army officer who had abandoned the family just one year after she was born. That desertion formed Taylor's negative opinion of white people and so she despised them and everything about them that she saw in herself, including her hazel eyes, light skin, and silken curls.

For a while, in order to combat the part of her she hated, she overamplified her blackness; for years she only wore her hair in cornrows, and when those cheap gold door-knocker earrings fell out of style, Taylor continued to sport them with pride, because to her they felt unequivocally Black with a capital B.

She attended Howard University even though she had also been accepted to Yale. As a college student, Taylor was active in several Black Power organizations, and she graduated as a member of the Delta Sigma Theta sorority.

It took decades, but eventually Taylor made peace with her European DNA, so much so that after years of rejecting Caucasian suitors she finally stopped saying: *Hell to the no!* and dated a few white men.

But the revelation that her African brothers and sisters were practicing the same atrocities that white men had engaged in centuries earlier placed Taylor between a rock and a hard place. If she revived her hate and turned it on the Africans, on the very roots of who she claimed to be, then wouldn't she once again be hating one-half of herself?

She was old enough to know that hate didn't fix problems—it only made things worse.

Taylor began with sending hefty donations to church groups that helped the young women who had escaped the shrines. For a while, that sated her need to help, but soon she was worried that her dollars were not actually being spent efficiently. She'd read one article after the next about so-called charitable organizations hoarding donations for their own personal gain. One article alleged that only ten cents of every dollar donated made it to the intended recipients. That little slice of knowledge had come as a shock to her, and while Taylor didn't completely cut her purse strings with the church groups, she did reduce the amounts she donated.

Her epiphany came while watching a documentary on Mahatma Gandhi. The next day, his words still pulsing in her mind, Taylor walked into her office at IBM, sat down at her desk, and stared at the blank screen of her computer monitor until her secretary brought her a cup of coffee and asked if she was feeling okay.

"Yes, yes, I'm just fine. I'm better than fine," Taylor said, and then stood up, gathered her things, and left.

A day later she put her Midtown apartment on the market, sold her car, emptied her savings account, cashed in her stocks, and closed her 401(k). It was only then that she called Allen and told him what she had done.

Allen was flabbergasted. "What? You're kidding me, right?"

"Nope!"

"Are you having a mental breakdown?"

"No, I'm having a break*through*."

Taylor was forty-seven years old and childless, with no prospects of marriage. Her mother was deceased. She did have several cousins in the Midwest with whom she exchanged Christmas cards, but otherwise there was little communication.

She had made a lot of money in her position as a director at IBM, but money was overrated, and it hadn't bought her love or fulfillment. So what was she really doing with herself besides working toward an early grave? She always knew there was more to life than what met the eye, but she never in a million years thought that *more* would be thousands of miles away in Ukemby.

"So you're just going to move to Africa? Just like that?" Allen asked.

"People do it every day."

"It's all so sudden. What brought this on?"

"Mahatma Gandhi said something like, *Be the change that you wish to see in the world*, and I'm going to do just that!"

Of course she convinced him to come along—after Allen weighed the pros and cons, the pros won out. After all, he was between relationships and his dream of becoming a world-renowned artist was a long time coming. And while he loved teaching art to middle-school children in the San Francisco public school system, as of late he was finding it less inspiring and more and more stifling.

But still . . . Africa was so far away and so foreign.

Taylor had pressed: "You don't have to stay forever, just come and experience it. I think it might change your life. It certainly changed mine."

They spent the winter traveling around the country, communing with the people, and absorbing the culture.

Allen became especially fascinated with the names of the shops and the colorful adornments displayed on the buses, taxis, and *tro-tros*.

Only God Knows Provisions and Cosmetics
All for the Lord Hamburgers and Franks
No Jesus, No Life. Know Jesus, Know Life!
Chastity Is a Lifestyle

When the time came for Allen to return to the States, he looked at Taylor and stated, "Maybe I'll extend my visa for another month and spend the spring here with you." That extension had led to another, and then a letter to the board of education explaining that he would not be returning in the fall, but hoped to see them the following winter. Then a new Ukemban summer arrived and Allen was still there.

Taylor never imagined herself the type of person to live in the country. She fancied herself a city girl, but when she and Allen decided that they would spend a week in the eastern part of Ukemby known as the Zolta region, Taylor found herself seduced by the lush countryside and fell head over heels in love with a ten-acre plot of land located just outside of Ketak.

The property was forested with acacia and baobab trees. The grass was a stunning emerald green sprinkled with wildflowers. There was a dilapidated mud hut and a well that provided fresh drinking water.

"It looks like an oasis," Allen swooned.

She purchased it for a little over fifteen thousand cendi, approximately ten thousand US dollars. To celebrate, the friends splurged on an overpriced bottle of South African champagne, took it back to the property, and drank it beneath the evening sun.

"So what are you going to call it?" Allen asked.

Taylor thought for a moment. The only name that fit was the word that came to mind when she'd first laid eyes on the land: "Eden."

Allen nodded. "Good name. What are you going to build on it?"

Taylor rested her head on his shoulder. "A life."

That was nearly three years ago and now Allen was calling her name and waving his hand in her face: "Taylor? Earth to Taylor!"

She jerked back to reality, abruptly stood up, snatched the glass jug of water from the table, and marched from the shade of the eatery directly toward Abeo.

"Here you go," Taylor offered, thrusting the jug at her.

Abeo took a step back. Her eyes dropped briefly to the jug before she shook her head and inched bashfully away.

Taylor followed her. "Please, take it. I know you are thirsty. At least give some water to your baby."

Abeo's frightened eyes drifted over to the driver who was already charging toward them.

"Hey you!" the man called out.

Taylor whirled around. "What?"

The young man was taken aback by the fearlessness on Taylor's face. "You, miss, you want to buy something or what?"

"No."

"Then go away." He waved his hand in her face as if she were a mosquito.

Taylor pulled her shoulders back and stood her ground. "I will not." She turned to Abeo again. "Please, please at least give the baby a few sips."

Abeo stood frozen, her eyes locked on the angry face of the driver.

"Hey lady," the driver stepped between them, "you are harassing my worker. Either buy something or piss off!"

"Worker? You mean *slave*, don't you?"

The driver took a menacing step toward Taylor. Her grip tightened around the jug. She so badly wanted to smash it into his face, but Allen was on her by then, pulling her backward by the shoulders.

"Come on, Taylor."

"Yeah, lady, listen to your boyfriend before you get hurt."

Taylor was quiet on the ride back to Eden. When Allen turned the car onto the road that led to the property, her mood seemed to lift and her eyes brightened. No matter how bad she felt, the beauty of the place never failed to astound and amaze her. The majestic baobab trees that lined either side of the road were in flower.

Allen steered the car with great caution, his eyes

watchful for the resident pets—two cats and three rag-
tag mutts. *Are you trying to build a women's shelter or a zoo?* Allen had joked when she brought the last dog home.

The first dormitory of Taylor's shelter was completed,
a simple cinder-block building comprising eight bedrooms. The second building, which would house the
classrooms, was currently under construction.

Allen pulled the car to a stop and he and Taylor
climbed out.

Abdula, a tall, sinewy Muslim, appeared from behind the completed building. He was carrying a machete; his dark skin shimmered with perspiration.

Allen raised his hand in greeting.

"Hello, Abdula," Taylor cried. "How goes it today?"

Abdula responded in his broken English, "Everything is good. You come and see."

There were three other men working at clearing the
field behind the buildings. They were using nothing but
their machetes, and the land looked as clean as if it had
been cleared with machines.

"Beautiful!" Taylor squealed.

Abdula grinned.

Allen clapped him warmly on the back. "Thank you
very much, Abdula."

"So we will see you again in the morning, yes?"

"Yes."

Allen and Taylor had already renovated the mud hut
that came with the land. The space doubled as their
sleeping quarters and office. They slept in hammocks
instead of beds. Tacked to the walls were photographs
Taylor had taken of various *trokosi* shrines as well as a
map of the greater Zolta region where more than seventy

shrines were known to exist. The ones Taylor planned to target were circled in red.

Back at the shrine, Abeo carefully slipped her nipple from Pra's mouth. He was fast asleep, his body twitching with dreams. She laid him down on the mat and covered him with a worn blanket. All she could think of was the woman who'd approached her in Aboão. She replayed the encounter and recalled the details: the woman's face, her lips, the curl of her hair, her painted fingernails, and the condensation on the jug she'd held out to her.

Abeo went to the tiny window of her hut and gazed out at the moon. She'd watched it so many times but it had never affected her in the way it did at that moment. Something soft moved in her chest and she brought her hand to her heart. It had been a long time since she'd felt this sensation; even so, she recognized it immediately as the flutter of butterflies. It was, Ismae once shared with her, the joy she'd felt behind her navel when Abeo was just an embryo.

Abeo still became sad when she thought about her parents, but for some reason on that day, the memory of her mother elated her. And for a brief moment, that joy felt very much like freedom.

EDEN REHABILITATION CENTER
KETAK, UKEMBY

28

The priest popped a kola nut into his mouth and crunched it between his teeth. He studied the bottle of schnapps Allen had given him and then set it down on the ground at his feet. He looked at Allen and used his chin to gesture toward the platter of kola nuts.

Allen raised his hand. "No, but thank you."

In the corner of the hut was a twenty-inch television turned on its side and covered in fine red dirt. The priest saw Allen staring and flung his hand at it. "Heh, it was a gift from a family. What am I supposed to do with it? We have no electricity here. So I use it as a table."

"That makes sense," Allen remarked.

"So now you want to take a girl? For what?"

Allen cleared his throat. "To offer her a chance to live freely."

The priest laughed. "Freely? Hmmmm, freeness is not always a good thing. Freeness is what brought many of these girls here in the first place, you know. Now they are paying for the so-called freeness of their family members and ancestors."

The priest plucked a second kola nut from the platter, thoughtfully examined it, and placed it in his mouth. His eyes moved to the open doorway; he seemed to be pondering something.

"There is a girl. She is sickly and a poor worker, not worth her weight in *gari*." He chuckled at his own wit. "The gods are not happy with her. I will let you have her for . . ." the priest's eyes rolled up to the thatched ceiling and then back to Allen, "one thousand cendi."

"One thousand cendi?"

"Yes."

Allen did a quick calculation in his head. It was nearly seven hundred US dollars. "I don't have that kind of money." He was starting to feel nauseous. It was a feeling that always came over him when he was negotiating a price for another human being. To say it was upsetting would be an understatement. To say that it made him angry enough to kill—that would be hitting the nail right on the head. Allen forced the bile back down his throat.

"Okay, okay, then I will give her to you for eight hundred cendi."

"No." Allen rubbed his cheek. "You told me she is sickly."

"Yes, okay, seven hundred."

"No."

In the end, he paid one hundred and twenty-five cendi for a fourteen-year-old girl named Eshi, who was frail, blind in one eye, and missing a foot.

29

With Pra on her hip, Abeo waded into the river. He dug his tiny fingers into her flesh and whimpered. Abeo cooed to him, uttering small words of comfort. When the water touched her knees, she peeled him from her body and lowered him until his toes were submerged. Pra squealed and curled his knees to his chest.

"No, Mama, no!" he cried.

Abeo ignored his objections and continued to lower him until the water covered most of his body. Pra became outraged—batting her face and kicking at her belly. Abeo made a game out of dunking him quickly into the water and then pulling him up and swinging him through the air. Pra shrieked in terror the first few times, but his squeals eventually turned into giggles and then laughter. Once his fear was forgotten, he paddled his feet and slapped happily at the surface of the water. When Abeo was done washing him, she took him back to the riverbank, set him down on the grass, and gave him two large stones that he clapped loudly together, laughing at the din he made.

Abeo returned to the river, moving into the deep center where she submerged her head. When she came up for air, three girls were standing on the bank screaming and pointing frantically down the river. Abeo's eyes went to the place where she'd left Pra, but only the two rocks remained.

Panic-stricken, Abeo swam toward where the girls were pointing. She caught sight of Pra's foot bobbing on top of the water; his little toes were stiff and splayed. Abeo lunged forward, screaming his name; she was just millimeters away from him when the current swept him out of her reach, pulling him farther downstream where the river bent left, creating a whirlpool that sucked Pra under.

Abeo dove, her eyes searching frantically for her son, but all she could see was a wavy wall of darkness. She came up and then dove again.

On the riverbank, the girls who'd first sounded the alarm now stood silent, staring mournfully at the dark, swirling water.

The current wrapped its fingers around Abeo's calves and tugged.

The muddy bottom slipped beneath her feet and she crumpled into the water. Abeo opened her mouth and allowed the river to drain in.

30

Taylor looked in the mirror and saw a gray hair. It didn't upset her; in fact, it made her happy because she took it as a reminder of all the life she had lived thus far.

She had recruited quite a few volunteers who shared her revulsion for the practice of ritual servitude, as well as her vision for Eden. Donations of food, clothing, and furniture trickled in from the surrounding communities and finally, after years of writing letters and making phone calls, a small Wisconsin newspaper ran a story about the plight of the *trokosi*. That story was picked up by the *Chicago Tribune* and then the *Daily Mirror*.

Back in 1996, Taylor had accompanied a congregation of religious leaders and women's-rights advocates to Port Masi to address Parliament about the practice of ritual servitude. Two years later, the Ukemban government passed a law banning all forms of it.

Taylor expected the government to put together a task force. She imagined groups of men dressed in black, brandishing automatic weapons, swooping down on the shrines, arresting the priests and freeing the girls. But that expectation turned out to be a fantasy, because the practice remained alive and well. Apparently, the law was just a few words on a piece of paper that the government had no intention of actually enforcing.

The Eden Rehabilitation Center, as it was known, was home to twenty girls under the age of eighteen. They'd all arrived physically, mentally, spiritually, and emotionally damaged. Some of them wept day and night, others wet the bed and experienced night terrors. One girl walked in her sleep—Taylor often found her standing in a nearby field unable to explain how she'd gotten there.

Their experiences with the opposite sex had been vile and terrifying, and had left them with a deep fear of men. Because of this, all the on-site volunteers at Eden were women. Allen was the exception, because he was somewhat effeminate and not at all intimidating.

During their stay they were provided with medical care, three well-balanced meals, and lessons on language, spelling, arithmetic, cloth weaving, sewing, cooking, and hairdressing.

No matter what job Taylor assigned a volunteer to do, it was understood that it was *everyone's* responsibility to shower constant praise, encouragement, and love onto the girls in order to allay their fears and rebuild their self-esteem. Taylor made it her personal business to tell them each and every day that she loved them.

Not everybody in Ukemby was happy with what Taylor and Allen were doing. Some people saw it as sacrilegious. Rocks had been pelted through the dormitory windows and foul words spray-painted on the walls of the buildings. The tires on Taylor's truck had been slashed several times, and threatening letters arrived almost daily.

"This is what happens when you interfere with tradition," an officer warned when Taylor called the police after vandals had set fire to one of the huts.

She realized right then and there that her complaints would be filed in the trash, the assailants would never be pursued, and possibly they would even be encouraged. And after that realization, she bought a gun.

31

The shrine was four miles off a secondary road, tucked behind a thicket of plantain trees. Allen pulled the truck over to the side of the road, grabbed the bottle of schnapps from the passenger seat, and climbed out. He raised his hand in greeting to a man who stood watching him from the opposite side of the road. When the man did not respond, Allen offered a smile, took a deep breath, and made his approach.

"Good day, my name is Allen and I'm looking for the priest," he offered in his practiced Wele.

The man scrutinized him before asking, "What is your business with him?"

This part was always tricky. "My family has suffered some misfortunes as of late . . . I have a daughter . . . she is nine years old."

The man turned and called to a group of women who were squatting down on their haunches weaving mats. One scurried over and Allen was instructed to follow her, but instead she fell into step behind him.

She directed him down an uneven footpath. When Allen turned around to check that she was still behind him, she urged him onward.

When Allen reached the hut, the woman hurried

around him and rushed inside. A moment later, she reappeared and beckoned him in.

To Allen, the priests had all started to resemble one
another. He supposed that this was his own fault. He'd
stopped seeing their faces ages ago. This one, however,
seemed younger than the others.

Allen handed him the bottle of schnapps. The priest
took it and offered him a seat.

Allen reeled off the monologue he had committed to
memory: "Let me first apologize for obtaining an audience with you under false circumstances. The truth is
that I am coming to you to ask if you might find it in
your heart to release one of your girls. Maybe someone
who is no longer of use to you, someone who is more of
a burden than an asset . . ."

Duma listened to the black American drone on. He
had heard about this man who traveled from shrine to
shrine, relieving priests of their *trokosi*. He'd heard there
was a white-looking American woman as well.

"What do you do with them after you bring them to
this center of yours?"

"We educate them, teach them a skill, ease them
back into society, and find them work."

Duma chuckled. "Why?"

They always asked this. "Because *our* god has asked
us to do this."

Duma didn't have an ounce of respect for Allen or
his god. As far as he was concerned, this American was
nothing more than a garbage collector there to relieve
him of his damaged and useless goods.

"I have one girl . . ." He paused for a moment and
then said simply, "Her mind is gone." He looked at Allen

for a reaction, but there was none, so he continued in a matter-of-fact tone: "She will probably die soon. She's stopped eating and barely works her weight in *gari*. You buying her will save me the trouble of having to bury her. I will sell her to you for one hundred cendi and," he pointed to Allen's wrist, "that watch."

32

Not even death wanted her, so it sent the devil to pull her from it. Duma had dragged Abeo to shore and pumped her chest until she spewed water.

After that, there was coughing and then darkness.

That was some years ago, but the loss of her son had left Abeo hollow; now, when she breathed, the air rattled around inside of her like gravel in an empty can.

When Allen presented Abeo to Taylor, she looked at Abeo's emaciated, sore-covered body and thought that she was the most pitiful thing she'd ever seen. Taylor had to turn her face away because she didn't want Abeo to see her tears.

She took Abeo by the hand and led her to the bathhouse, where she removed the young woman's dress and guided her into the shower stall. When Taylor turned the silver knob on the wall, the water gushed out and Abeo's head snapped up, her arms shooting into the air; she opened her mouth and the scream that boomed out stood Taylor's hair on end.

Taylor then took Abeo to the sink and spent the next hour gently removing the layers of dirt from her body. When she was done, Abeo was a different color. Taylor applied salve to the sores, parted Abeo's lips and carefully brushed her teeth, and then dressed her in a new nightgown and put her to bed. She thought about Abeo all through the night and went to the dormitory before sunrise to check on her. Fatuma, a fourteen-year-old girl who had been at Eden for over a year, met Taylor at the door.

"The smaller girls are afraid of her," Fatuma whispered. "She sleeps with her eyes open."

Three months later, Abeo still remained mute and indolent. The other girls tried hard to include her in their hand-clapping games. They demonstrated the clapping for her, and then picked up her hands and brought them together. But when they released them, Abeo's arms dropped back down to her sides like weights. In the classroom, she either gazed unblinking at nothing or pressed her forehead against the desk and stared at the grooves in the wood.

One day Allen went into town for supplies and came back with an old VCR and a fifteen-inch color television. The casings around both were scratched and dented. He also had a box of dusty videotapes.

"Where did you get all this?" Taylor asked, amused.

"Shiloh gave them to me."

"Shiloh? The man who takes donated clothes and sells them on the black market?"

"The very same."

"I love it," Taylor laughed. "A criminal with a heart of gold." She started digging through the box of tapes. "*The Sound of Music*, *101 Dalmatians*, *Snow White*. This is great, Allen. The girls are really going to enjoy this."

Some of the girls had been born into villages that were so isolated, they'd never seen a television, or white people, and so they watched the movies in amazement as Taylor did her best to translate the dialogue.

One night they gathered in the classroom to watch *The Wizard of Oz*. Taylor popped the cassette into the VCR and pressed play. A few moments later, the screen exploded in Technicolor accompanied by the movie studio's introductory music.

Minutes into the film, Taylor looked over to find that Abeo was watching intently. Eyes wide, the girl had inched her bottom to the very edge of the chair, her fingers slowly gathering the material of her skirt until it was a ball in her clenched fists. In the darkness, Taylor could see Abeo's lips moving soundlessly along with the dialogue.

An idea sparked in Taylor's mind. While she had never been educated on the mysterious workings of the human mind, she did believe in following her instincts and they had rarely led her down a wrong path.

So the next day, Taylor removed Abeo from the regular roster of classes, took her into a quiet room, and set her down to watch the movie that had brought the only bit of light in her that anyone had seen since her arrival.

Over the following week, Taylor played the movie so many times that the plastic cogs of the cassette squealed. But with each viewing, Abeo showed more signs of life and Taylor could barely contain her excitement.

One morning, as the girls sat enjoying their breakfast of *kenkey* and fish, Abeo—who until that moment had to be fed, washed, dressed, like an infant—pushed away the fork of food that hovered inches from her mouth, and stood up.

Taylor was in her office when she heard Halima, the cook, yelling for her to come quick.

When Taylor laid a cautious hand on her shoulder, Abeo flinched, turned a bashful eye in her direction, and asked in a childlike voice, "Where am I?"

"You're at Eden. Don't you remember coming here?"

Abeo offered her a vacant look.

Taylor took the young woman to her office and sat her down in a chair. "I am Taylor Adams and this is the Eden Rehabilitation Center."

Abeo glanced around, squeezed her eyes shut, and tried to remember, but she couldn't.

"What do you remember?"

"I remember . . ." she started in a faint voice, "my house. My parents and baby brother."

Taylor asked her a series of questions and Abeo was able to recall in vivid detail her life before she was taken to the shrine. The shrine and the years she'd spent there, however, had fallen into a black well in her memory.

"Do you know how old you are?"

Abeo thought about it and then responded: "Nine." What her mind could not handle, it had simply erased.

"I'm not sure exactly how old you are, but you're certainly not nine."

Abeo was perplexed.

"Come with me."

Abeo followed Taylor across the office to a full-length mirror propped up against the wall.

"See?" Taylor pointed at Abeo's reflection.

A grown woman stared back at her. She was tall, dark, and thin, with wide, dull eyes. Abeo moved closer, reached her arm out, and touched the hand of her mirrored self. "That's me?" she whispered in wonder.

"Yes, it is."

Abeo had many questions, and over the next few days Taylor tried her best to answer them.

"You keep talking about the shrine; why would my parents send me there?"

Taylor didn't know how to explain ritual servitude to a grown woman trapped in the mind of a nine-year-old. "They thought it was the best thing to do at the time." She had a few questions of her own. "Do you know how you got those marks on your body?"

Abeo did not, and when she tried to remember, her temples thumped. "When can I see my parents?" she asked.

Taylor wanted more than anything for Abeo to be reunited with her parents, but she knew from experience that those reunions were often traumatic.

Taylor grabbed a pad and pen from her desk. "Okay, Abeo, tell me their full names, your last known address, and your telephone number."

Abeo recited their names and her address with the unique gusto that only little children possess. She struggled with the telephone number before giving up and shamefully admitting, "I can't remember."

"That's okay. We'll find them with what we have."

Taylor sent a letter to the address Abeo had given her and it came back two weeks later with the word *Moved* scrawled on the front of the envelope.

"Can you think of anyone else? A cousin or uncle?"

Abeo chewed her bottom lip. "No," she squeaked.

33

A white woman named Fannie Horowitz who lived in New Mexico had read about what Taylor was doing in Ukemby and began sending money on a monthly basis. Two hundred dollars—exactly one-quarter of the amount she received from her dead husband's pension. Each month, Taylor responded with a handwritten thank you note.

In the most recent donation, Fannie had included a two-page letter written in pink ink and scented with talcum powder. In the letter she explained that she was a widow and that her children had made lives for themselves in various parts of the country. She only saw them and her grandchildren during the Christmas holidays. Most of her friends had died or were infirm, leaving her quite lonely.

Fannie wrote, *I am ashamed to say that I am counting the days until I die even though I consider myself to be a very young 68-year-old.* She'd drawn a smiley face after that sentence and Taylor didn't know whether she should laugh or cry for the woman.

> *I started making jewelry to fill the long hours of the day and I have discovered that it is very freeing and please excuse me for being forward, but do you think the young ladies would*

*like to learn to make jewelry? I'd like to come and teach
the girls to make jewelry. It is very therapeutic and I have
found that while I'm doing it, I forget about my age and the
circumstances that accompany it and I just think about the
beauty I am creating. If I did not have this hobby of mine,
I am sure I would have already succumbed to my miseries,
which are far less than what your girls have been through.
The truth is, I've never traveled out of the country, and Africa is not a place I have ever felt I wanted to visit, but now
Africa, Ukemby, and your girls are all I can think about. I
know it sounds crazy but I hope you understand.*

Taylor did understand.

Fannie had written: *I'd like to come and teach the girls to
make jewelry*—but Taylor knew she actually meant: *I'd like
to come and learn to love life again.*

By the time Fannie's supplies arrived, one month ahead
of her own arrival, Abeo had been at Eden for one year,
three months, and seven days.

Fannie had sent four big boxes filled with spools of
wire, jigs, round-nose and bent-nose pliers, wire cut-
ters, string, clasps, and dozens of clear plastic bags filled
with a variety of gemstones, beads, and baubles.

Taylor asked Abeo and two other girls to help her
sort through the items. The girls wondered at the strange
tools and swooned over the pretty pebbles. Abeo was
especially fascinated with a bag of pale-blue stones.

Taylor quickly addressed the curiosity in Abeo's
eyes: "They're called turquoise."

Abeo placed the bag of turquoise stones onto the
shelf and returned to the box, but her eyes kept wan-

dering back to them. The harder she tried to fight the attraction, the louder her heart banged in her chest.

"What is it? What's wrong?" Taylor asked.

Abeo pointed at the bag of stones and opened her mouth to speak, but only ragged breaths of air emerged. Memories had begun to come through—names, faces, places, and events. The good, the bad, and the wicked— all showered down on her in torrential sheets of recall.

Abeo pressed her hands to her head, declaring, "I remember now. It began with the ring . . ."

It began with the ring and ended with the death of Pra—after that day she'd fallen into a deep sleep and had woken up two years later at Eden, with the scent of *kenkey* and fish in her nostrils.

Taylor's mouth hung slack with shock as she listened to Abeo's rapid narrative. Taylor knew very little about the girls' individual experiences because they usually avoided discussing their painful pasts. But now Abeo was painting a candid portrait of the dreadfulness they'd all experienced, and as Taylor listened, she realized that she could never in a million years have imagined the very worst of it—and it was those parts that she would never ever be able to shake loose, because they'd broken off in her heart like a stake.

34

Thema set her teacup down into the sink and glanced at her wristwatch. It was just past seven and she should have been out of the house fifteen minutes ago; now she would be late for work. She checked her purse for her car keys and was standing at the door when the telephone rang. Thema peered down at her watch—the time was ticking away, so she decided to let the machine pick up.

She was halfway out the door when the beep sounded and she heard the raspy voice of a stranger say: *"This is Taylor Adams. I'm trying to reach Thema Wusu, a family member of Abeo Kata."*

Abeo Kata?

Thema was sure she'd heard wrong, but ran to the phone anyway, leaving the door standing wide open.

"Hello? Hello?" she panted into the receiver.

"Good morning, I'm looking for Thema Wusu."

"Yes, yes, that's me. Did you say something about Abeo?"

"Yes, I have Abeo here at the Eden Rehabilitation Center in Ketak and—"

"You have Abeo? Abeo Kata?" Thema tightened her grip on the phone and planted her back against the wall to keep from falling over.

"Yes, Abeo Kata."

Thema shook her head. "I-I . . . don't believe it. And you are who again?"

Taylor was used to the reaction. The first contact always took the relation by surprise. Taylor began again, this time speaking very slowly: "My name is Taylor Adams. I run the Eden Rehabilitation Center in Ketak—"

"A rehabilitation center?"

"Yes, for former *trokosi*."

It was all very surreal—the first call and the one that followed later that evening. When Thema heard Abeo's grown-up voice on the other end of the line saying, "Hello, Auntie," she thought she would never stop crying.

Weeks later, one bright Sunday afternoon, Thema and her husband Joseph made the drive to Ketak. Thema was so anxious and nervous that she chewed her thumbnails down to the nubs.

A simple wooden sign nailed to a tree announced that they were now entering Eden. Joseph drove the car slowly past mud huts and cinder-block buildings with walls decorated with painted images of flowers, running vines, and smiling children.

Girls of all ages, holding hands or clutching dolls and books to their chests, strolled around the compound. At least two girls, from what Thema could see, were on crutches and one moved around with the aid of a sensing stick.

"Which one is it?" Joseph asked as he inched the car closer to the main buildings.

"I think that one." Thema pointed to the canvas sign over the doorway that read, WELCOME.

Two teenage girls wearing simple white cotton smocks greeted them at the door and handed them each a program. The older of the two girls was missing an ear, and Thema found herself unable to pull her eyes away from the gaping hole on the side of her head. Joseph caught her staring and nudged her in the ribs.

Once inside the building, they were met by a tall, willowy young woman with an infectious smile. "Welcome, my name is Naja," she said. "Please follow me."

She led them down a hallway of classrooms that were empty save for chairs, desks, and various commendations taped to the walls. Thema and Joseph followed her into a large classroom where a dozen or so guests were already seated and waiting.

"The ceremony will begin in just a little while," Naja announced before leaving them.

Guests continued to stream in until only standing room remained. The air grew thick with the scent of colognes and perfumed lotions. The heat felt like straight pins on their skin and people shifted uncomfortably and impatiently in their chairs, throats were cleared, and the thin paper programs were put to use as fans.

Thema fidgeted with excitement. She checked her watch and crossed and uncrossed her legs a dozen times. She was about to stand up when Taylor rushed into the room dressed in a traditional scoop-neck purple-and-green frock.

Taylor bubbled, "So sorry for the delay, ladies and gentlemen . . ."

Thema was struck by the woman's appearance. She was shorter, wider, and lighter-complexioned than her voice had let on.

"I had a little problem I needed to attend to in town. But I'm here now and I hope you accept my sincere apologies . . . Oh my goodness! It's so wonderful to have you here with us today!" Taylor went on to share the story of how Eden came to be, how many girls had been rehabilitated since its inception, and the plans she had for its future. Then she clapped her hands. "So, without further delay, I would like to introduce Eden's graduates . . ."

She called the girls by name and they filed in one by one. They varied in height, scale, and hue. Some wore their hair cut close to their scalps and others sported braided styles. They were all dressed in white jumpers with handmade purple-and-yellow butterfly broaches pinned to the bodices of their dresses.

When Taylor called Abeo's name, Thema shot to her feet. She strained to see around the large headdress worn by the woman in front of her, who had also stood up. When Abeo turned to face the audience, Thema raised a trembling hand and waved.

Abeo saw Thema and her entire face broke into a smile.

After the ceremony, Thema rushed to Abeo, threw her arms around her neck, and hugged her tighter than Abeo could ever remember being hugged in her life.

The last time Thema had seen her, she was a happy little girl. Now. Well, now they were both women, with histories and battle scars and more than a little touch of sadness in their eyes.

Hand in hand, Abeo and Thema moved toward the white tents where the reception was being held.

A soft afternoon breeze rustled the palms and a new

litter of mewling kittens followed their mother away from the crowd of strangers and into the tall grass.

Thema couldn't stop staring and every so often she'd raise her hand and run her fingers along the neat corn-rows that lined Abeo's scalp. "You've grown into such a beautiful young woman," she commented over and over again.

Joseph, who had said very little up to that point, clutched his plastic cup of lemonade, rocked back on his heels, and nodded in agreement.

There was so much to say, but there would be plenty of time for that. For now they would just enjoy the day, enjoy one another, and wait for the years that separated them to flake away.

35

O n the drive to Port Masi, Thema rode in the backseat with Abeo, holding her hand and catching
her up on her life. "I'm a grandmother now!" she
announced proudly.

When they arrived in the city, Abeo's posture
straightened. It seemed to Abeo that Port Masi had
swelled in size, that there were a great many more shops
and vendors lining the sidewalks and thousands more
people than she remembered. She turned to Thema and
asked, "May I roll down the window?"

"Of course!"

The scents and sounds of Port Masi rushed in, setting
all of Abeo's senses afire. "I'm home," she moaned softly.

"I remember your house!" she exclaimed when Joseph
turned the car into the driveway.

Once inside, Joseph carried Abeo's small suitcase
into his daughter's old room.

In the living room, Abeo gazed at the framed photographs that covered the walls. "Is that Ebony? Is that her
husband?"

Thema grinned. "Yes," she said, pointing at another
photo, "and those are their two children."

"Two?"

Thema nodded to another photo. "Yes, a boy named Ramla and a girl named Aisha."

"They are beautiful. They look like her."

"I think so too. Come, let me get this dinner heated up."

Abeo followed Thema into the kitchen. It wasn't as she remembered it. The walls were a different color and the appliances were silver, instead of the pale yellow from her youth.

"Can I help?"

"No, no, please just sit down. This will be ready in a minute." Thema poured the cold stew into the waiting pot, removed a box of matches from the shelf above the stove, and lit the pilot. "Would you like something to drink?"

"Yes, thank you."

"Do you still like orange soda?"

Abeo was touched that Thema remembered. "Yes, thank you, I do."

Dinner went smoothly as they deftly avoided the elephant in the room and instead discussed the growth of Port Masi as well as the people Abeo had known in her childhood. When the dishes were cleared and Joseph had retired to the living room, Thema placed the kettle on the stove, sat down, and reached for Abeo's hands. Their fingers locked.

"I'm so happy to have you here."

"I'm happy to be here, Auntie."

"Well, it seems we have a lot to talk about. But I don't know if we should tackle it today? Perhaps tomorrow would be best when we've both had a good night's rest. What do you think?"

Abeo didn't want to seem rude, but she had waited for so long to hear the truth. She didn't want to wait another minute and certainly not another day. "I was hoping we could talk . . . now."

Thema understood. "Of course, Abeo. When we spoke, I told you that Ismae and Wasik had moved, but that is not exactly the entire truth."

Suddenly, Thema's hand felt as hot as the screeching kettle.

When Thema released her hands to prepare the tea, Abeo sighed with relief.

Thema set the hot cup of tea before Abeo and lowered herself back into the chair. She gave Abeo a long, tender look. "The truth is," she started in a quivering voice, "and this is so very hard for me to say . . ."

"She's dead, isn't she?" Abeo whispered.

Thema was taken aback. "Uhm . . . yes. Yes, she is. I'm so sorry, Abeo. How did you know?"

Abeo wiped a tear from her cheek. "I don't know," she mumbled. "I just felt she was dead, because if she were alive she would have come looking for me. She would have come looking for me and she would have found me."

Who would it serve to tell Abeo that Ismae didn't search for her? The devil, that's who, and Thema had never been his disciple and wasn't going to start now.

"That's right, Abeo." Thema nodded.

"When did she . . . When did it happen?"

"A year or so after you left . . . I mean . . ."

"And Papa and Agwe, where are they?"

A shadow fell over Thema's face. She flicked an invisible crumb from the table. "He has taken a new wife."

"A new wife?" Abeo looked wounded.

"Yes. He has made a new life for himself and Agwe in Togo."

"And what of Grandmother?" Abeo asked.

Thema picked a piece of invisible lint from the table. "She died two years ago," she muttered.

Abeo took a moment to process the information. "Oh," she breathed, and then: "Will he see me?"

"Who?"

"Papa. Will Papa see me?"

"I don't know, Abeo . . ."

"Well, I will write him a letter and let him know that I forgive him and that I am still his daughter and even though he did this thing that was wrong, I still love him in spite of—"

Thema raised her hand. "He doesn't keep in touch with me, but I'm sure we can find someone who knows his address." Her tone was tight.

Abeo's voice brightened. "And what of Auntie Serafine?"

"Last I heard, she was well."

"Still living in America?"

"I guess so."

"Are you not in touch?"

"No, we're not."

"So, she doesn't know that I am . . . okay?"

Thema looked down at her fingers. "No, she does not."

Abeo eyed her. "Is there something else?"

Thema thought, *Am I so transparent?* "Come with me, Abeo. I want to show you something."

In Ebony's former bedroom, the white walls were

plastered with photographs that chronicled Ebony's life from childhood, through the purgatory of adolescence, and finally adulthood. Abeo felt a tinge of envy; the photographs were just another reminder of the time she'd lost.

Thema retrieved a mahogany jewelry box from a shelf in the closet and sat on the side of the bed, holding it in her lap. "There is something very important you need to know." She raised the lid and removed a thin green booklet.

Abeo studied the cover, which was embossed with gold letters that read: *United States of America.*

Thema handed it to her. "Open it."

Inside was a black-and-white photograph of a grinning toddler wearing gold ball earrings and a white barrette that clung to a tuft of dark hair. Below the picture was the name *Abeo Vinga.*

"Who is this?"

"It's you. You are Abeo Vinga."

Abeo blinked. "I don't understand. I am Abeo Kata."

"No, you're not. You are a Vinga."

Abeo looked at the picture again, closed the book, and turned it over in her hands. "I don't understand, isn't this an American passport?"

Thema realized that she was going about things in the wrong order. She set the box on the bed and folded her hands in her lap. "Okay, here it is. Wasik and Ismae are not your parents—they are your aunt and uncle. Serafine is your mother—"

The passport fell to the floor. "What is this you are telling me? Serafine is my mother?"

"Yes. Serafine became pregnant while she was attending school in America. She was very young and it was decided that she would have you and bring you here to Ukemby to be raised by Ismae and Wasik."

Abeo stood and backed away from Thema. "I don't believe it."

"It is done all the time."

Thema pointed at the passport. "Wasik gave it to me before he remarried. That and your birth certificate. He must have believed somewhere in his heart that one day someone would find you."

Abeo's back touched the wall. "And did she know they were going to do what they did to me?"

Thema shook her head. "Nobody knew. Not even Ismae. Wasik made that decision. When Serafine found out, she flew here to find you, but Wasik wouldn't tell her where he'd taken you." Thema rose from the bed, walked to Abeo, and placed her hands on the young woman's heaving shoulders. "We all tried to find you. We all did."

"And . . . and does she know that I am here with you now?" Abeo blubbered.

"No. I was being truthful before. We have not spoken for many years."

"Well, we have to tell her."

"Yes, of course."

NEW YORK CITY

2003

36

Serafine had to pee again. It was ridiculous because she'd gone twice before leaving the house, and then again when she'd first arrived at the airport. She looked down at her watch; the flight was due to land in less than twenty minutes. She could wait, she told herself, and crossed her legs. Her bladder ballooned. No, no she couldn't.

Afterward she stood at the white sink washing her hands, with her heart fluttering about in her chest like a hummingbird. How many years had it been? Ten? Twelve? Serafine had lost count. Never mind the years, what about the lies?

Serafine raised her eyes to the mirror. She'd gained quite a bit of weight. One very bad divorce, a pack-a-day smoking habit, a liter of vodka a week, a job she hated, a current husband she despised—all of that had taken its toll. The woman who gazed back at her was the end result of what seemed to be a cursed life.

She combed her fingers through her brittle hair and made a sucking sound. Why oh why had she streaked her hair blond? It made her look like a clown, like a woman trying to hang onto a youth that had fled years earlier.

Abeo would wonder what had happened to her

glamorous, beautiful Aunt Serafine. Not *aunt*, Serafine quickly corrected herself—*mother*.

It all seemed unreal to her, even though many months had passed since she'd received that first phone call, during the early-morning hours when the sky outside her window was still black. Serafine had reached for the receiver and braced herself. People only called at those hours when the news was bad. "Yes?" and a familiar voice called her name. Serafine said "Yes" again and waited.

"Serafine, this is Thema."

Serafine's anger returned and all of the old wounds sprang leaks.

"Serafine? Serafine, are you there?"

"Yes?" she responded icily.

"Abeo is here with me," Thema stated simply.

Serafine had sat up in her queen-size bed and clicked on the lamp. "Do you think you're funny? What kind of sick bitch are you, Thema? You waste your money to taunt me, just so you can hurt me . . . again?"

"Hold on," Thema said, and suddenly there was a new voice, a stranger's voice, calling, "Auntie? Auntie Serafine? This is Abeo."

Serafine still hadn't believed it. "Who is this? Why are you doing this?"

"I promise you, Auntie, this is not a joke, it's me. Abeo."

The voice sounded earnest, pleading, and bruised. Serafine gripped the phone with one hand, while the other thrashed through the nightstand drawer in search of her cigarettes.

Serafine had long resigned herself to the very real

possibility that Abeo was dead. Death was a finality she could deal with, because the idea that Abeo was alive and languishing somewhere in the bush—well, that was a notion that Serafine hadn't been mentally equipped to handle.

She slipped a cigarette between her lips, but her hand was trembling so badly that she couldn't get it lit.

The voice claiming to belong to Abeo said, "You remember one time you came to Ukemby on vacation and brought me a hamburger? A Big Mac, I think?"

Serafine croaked, "Abeo?"

"Yes, Auntie, it's really me."

After that conversation, Serafine had walked around in a daze for weeks. When the first letter came, she stared long and hard at the Ukemban stamp before bringing the envelope to her nose and sniffing it. Even though it had traveled thousands of miles, the scent of Ukemby was still strong on the paper.

The letter was written in the hand of a child; misspelled words were struck through and misspelled again. Abeo had included photographs of Thema (who had gained weight) and Joseph (who was balding). The one of Abeo stopped Serafine's heart cold, because she looked exactly as Serafine had at that age.

Now, in the arrivals hall at JFK Airport, Serafine elbowed herself through the crowd and stationed herself behind the metal barriers. Her breath caught in her throat each time the doors parted, releasing a swarm of travelers pushing carts piled high with boxes and suitcases that had been wrapped in so many layers of cellophane they resembled large cocoons.

Serafine was gripping the metal barrier so hard that

the blood drained from her fingers, turning her knuckles a ghostly white. The deluge of people trickled down to groups of two and three and still there was no sign of Abeo.

A slow panic rose in Serafine.

Suppose Abeo hadn't made the flight? Wouldn't Thema have called to tell her? Serafine pulled her cell phone from her purse. 5 MISSED CALLS flashed across the screen. She scrolled through the numbers but none of them belonged to Thema.

The doors parted again and a little girl appeared, accompanied by a flight attendant. "Abeo?" Serafine whispered, confused. *Of course that's not Abeo*, she laughed to herself. *You're losing your mind, Serafine.*

She so badly wanted a cigarette. A cigarette and a drink. She looked at her phone again and then at the wall of windows and was struck with the sudden urge to run, to escape out into the winter air and pretend she'd never received Thema's call.

Serafine was not ready to confront her past—nor was she ready to be confronted by it. The room warmed and spun. Her eyes twitched, the world went gray, and for a moment she thought she would pass out. She stumbled where she stood, bumping into a man with a kufi on his head.

He planted a steady hand on the small of her back. "Miss, are you okay?"

Serafine blinked at him. "Yes, yes. Excuse me, I just need some fresh air," and she set off toward the glass doors. The red exit sign beckoned her like a lighthouse. Her footsteps quickened.

Just feet from the doors, a little boy ran into her

path. Serafine tried to sidestep him, but he locked his arms around her legs, giggling.

Serafine looked wildly around for the boy's parents as she tried to peel him from her. But he held fast and the two spun in circles like a pair of drunken marionettes.

"Carl! Carl!" The little boy's chunky mother came rushing toward them, lugging an infant in her arms. "Carl, let the nice lady go. Sorry, ma'am, he doesn't mean any harm. Let go of the lady, Carl. Carl, let go!!"

And then Serafine heard her name echo behind Carl's mother. Her head spun and there was Abeo, wearing a green cable-knit sweater, brown docksiders, and denim jeans. She looked younger than her years and was as effortlessly stunning as Serafine used to be.

"Abeo?"

Abeo ran toward her with her arms spread wide. "Oh, Auntie Serafine!" She plowed into Serafine and the two hugged and kissed each other's wet cheeks.

When they separated, Serafine's lip trembled and the words that had been sitting at the top of her heart every moment since she'd received the phone call from Thema jumped out of her throat: "Do you hate me?"

"No. No, of course not."

This wasn't to say that Abeo didn't struggle with the hate. After Thema had shared the ugly truth with her, hate had become a constant companion. It was Taylor who had saved her from being swallowed by it. She said, "Abeo, the weak can never forgive; forgiveness is an attribute of the strong. You know who said that, Abeo?"

Of course she knew. It was on the wall of every classroom in Eden. "Mahatma Gandhi."

"Exactly! Are you weak, Abeo?"

At one time she had thought she was weak, but Taylor told her that weak people didn't survive all that Abeo had endured.

"No, I'm strong!"

In the parking lot, mother and daughter hoisted Abeo's suitcase into the trunk of Serafine's six-year-old Saab. Serafine was so nervous that she rolled the car right past the silver box that held a wide-eyed parking attendant. When she realized her error, she brought her foot down hard on the brake and the nose of the car softly bumped the wooden arm that blocked the exit.

On the Belt Parkway, Serafine reached for the pack of cigarettes in the center console. She lowered the window, flooding the car with cold air, and Abeo's teeth began to chatter.

"Oh, sorry 'bout that." Serafine fiddled with a button on the control panel until the inside of the car pulsed with heat. "So," she started after she'd taken a few puffs of the cigarette, "how was the flight?"

"It was . . ." Abeo searched her hands for the right words, "scary at first. Being up so high above the clouds. And then it was okay, but the turbulence—"

Serafine's cell phone rang. She plucked it from the cup holder and pressed it to her ear. For ten minutes she jabbered on about work and some woman she referred to as "that high-rolling bitch." Abeo watched the road, waiting for Serafine to say something about her, something like, *I just picked my daughter up from the airport.* But she didn't mention Abeo at all and simply ended the call with, "No, I don't have any plans, I'm just going home to crash."

The silence enwrapped them. Serafine turned the radio on and lit another cigarette.

The atmosphere was awkward. Thema had warned Abeo that it would be. *It's been so many years*, she'd said. *You'll have to get to know one another again, and that will take time.*

Abeo stared out at the gray day. The trees were naked and the grass was a brittle brown carpet. New York was a stark contrast to the vibrantly colored world she'd departed just eleven hours earlier.

Serafine tossed the cigarette butt out the window, turned the volume down on the radio, and casually announced, "Um, just so you know, Abeo, I haven't told my husband that you are my . . . my . . ." The word *daughter* stuck in her throat like a pit and so Serafine avoided it altogether. "He thinks you're my niece. There wasn't enough time to explain all the details to him, but I will . . ."

She'd had months to prepare her husband. Abeo felt the hurt creep across her heart.

"Also, he doesn't know about the *other* thing."

The slavery? Abeo so wanted to spit, but instead she muttered, "It's okay, Auntie." Even though it wasn't.

37

The house was a cozy Cape Cod with a gray flagstone front. Two bedrooms, a study, living room, eat-in kitchen, and tiny dining room.

Serafine took her into the study. "The couch pulls out into a bed. The mattress is a bit uncomfortable, but I'll buy you a feather bed next week." She sighed. "I would put you in a bedroom, but we only have two and I'm in one and, well . . . he sleeps in the other."

Serafine's jaw tensed as she braced herself for a barrage of questions. But Abeo asked nothing.

The front door opened and Serafine rolled her eyes. "That's him now."

Abeo followed her into the kitchen where Ottley was standing over the counter flipping through the day's mail.

Serafine greeted him with a stiff, "Hey."

Ottley was tall, slender, and brown. When he turned and saw Abeo standing beside his wife, he smiled, revealing a row of crooked teeth.

"Well hello, you must be Abeo." He walked around Serafine and presented his hand.

Abeo barely touched him. She was strong, yes, but her strength did nothing to waylay the distress she felt when she was around members of the opposite sex.

Ottley slowly lowered his hand to his side. "I'm glad that you're . . . um, here and reunited with Serafine." He paused, then added, "I'm very sorry about your mother."

Abeo mumbled, "Thank you."

Ottley looked at Serafine. "So, shall we celebrate this reunion and maybe go out for a bite to eat?"

Go out to dinner and pretend to be the happy all-American family? Serafine didn't have the energy to play pretend. Their marriage was over; they were just waiting for the attorneys to sort through the grimy details of their pending divorce.

"Maybe another time, Ottley. Abeo has already had a very full day. I think we'll just order in."

Ottley looked relieved. "Whatever you say," he grunted, then looked over to Abeo. "It was very nice to meet you."

Abeo nodded.

"I have to get back to work, Serafine." Ottley reached for his keys.

"Yeah," Serafine replied sarcastically, "*work.*"

Serafine dodged the inevitable by identifying the five dishes and the condiments from a local Chinese restaurant. Abeo listened and tried hard to look interested, but she couldn't care less about soy sauce and chopsticks; she wanted to know who her father was and why Serafine had given her up. She'd heard Thema's version, but she wanted the story directly from her mother's mouth.

At the kitchen table, Abeo picked over her food in between sips from a can of Pepsi. Serafine took two bites of her egg foo yong and then pushed it aside in favor of the tall etched glass filled with vodka and tonic.

Abeo also set her food aside after a few bites. "Thank you, Auntie. It was very good."

"I'm glad you enjoyed it." Serafine coughed between pulls of her Marlboro. "I, um . . ." she mashed the tip of her cigarette into the ceramic ashtray, "I have something for you. Let me get it." She went to her bedroom and returned with a photo album. The pages were filled with shots taken during her visits to Ukemby. "Do you remember this?" She pointed to a photograph of Abeo dressed in pink-and-purple culottes, posed with one hand on her hip. Didi stood smiling in the background.

Abeo traced her finger over her glossy face. "I do." Of course she remembered the photo; it was taken the summer before her life was snatched away from her. She flipped through pages stopping here and there to gaze at images that unearthed one happy memory after the next.

"Oooh," Serafine moaned when they were halfway through the album. "That," she crooned slyly, "is Chipo Hama."

Abeo squinted at the image of the tall chocolate man with a sculpted Afro and dimpled chin. "Uhm, he lived down the street from us. I remember Mr. Hama."

Serafine leaned back in her chair. "Yes, Chipo had a major crush on me." She giggled like a schoolgirl.

The album held so many photos, and each one told a story. Flipping through it was like turning the pages of a history book.

"It's yours to keep."

Abeo's eyes lit up. "Really?"

Serafine grinned. The glow on her daughter's face made her feel good. "Yes, of course."

But then Abeo asked a question that Serafine was not expecting: "Do you have any photos of my father?"

"What?"

"What's my father's name?"

"What?" Serafine bleated a second time. Flustered, she instinctively reached for her cigarettes. "Well, I— uhm . . ." she stammered, violently shaking the empty cigarette pack. "Damnit," she muttered, crushing the pack and dropping it onto the table. "Well, you're grown up now and I guess you have a right to know." Serafine took a sip of her drink. "He was just some boy," she lied. "A boy named . . ." She paused and rolled her eyes to the ceiling, pretending to sift through her memory. "Smith. Yes, Charles Smith."

"Charles Smith?" Abeo cooed. "Charles Smith . . . Abeo Smith." She fused his fictional surname to her own. "Abeo Smith," she uttered again.

Serafine averted her eyes and took another sip of her drink.

"Does he know about me?"

The hopefulness in Abeo's voice was a knife in Serafine's back. She did not want to think about that time or that man. *Why,* she raged to herself, *is Abeo forcing me back into the past?* "No, no, he doesn't," she quipped, staring at her cuticles.

The light went out of Abeo's eyes and she slumped a little in her chair. "Did you love him?"

Serafine sighed. "Love? I was a child. Much younger than you are now. What do children know of romantic love? I was just young and foolish."

"And that's why you gave me to my mother, because you were so young?" Abeo questioned calmly. After be-

208 • PRAISE SONG FOR THE BUTTERFLIES

ing in the shrine for so many years, she didn't believe
that being young was a legitimate excuse for giving up
one's child. She'd known twelve-year-olds who gave
birth and went on to rear and love their children under
far-less-than-desirable circumstances.

"It wasn't my decision, Abeo. My parents decided for
me. You can't blame me for something I had no control
over." Serafine stood, walked to the sink, and peered
out of the window. "If I could go back in time, I would
change many things, but I can't and neither can you. We
just have to move forward and try to make the best of
now."

38

A few weeks into Abeo's stay, Serafine introduced her to her friends. They were a motley crew of middle-aged women who drove shiny cars and wore fake hair that they constantly stroked, smoothed, and twirled.

"So this is Abeo?" each one exclaimed when Serafine made the introduction. They spoke loudly to Abeo, as if she was hard of hearing.

"Nice to meet you!"

"Do you like America?!"

"Oooh, I love that accent of yours. So international!"

In the living room they gorged themselves on cocktail franks, cheese puffs, and crudités, and tried not to stare at Abeo as if she was an exhibit, even though Serafine treated her like she was.

"My Wele is so bad," Serafine sang in a high-pitched voice. "I hardly remember any of it," she lied. "But Abeo can speak it perfectly. Go ahead, Abeo, say . . ."

Later, as the women prepared to leave, one of them caught Abeo by the arm. "You must get this all the time, but my goodness if you don't look like that model Alek Wek. You're not as dark as she is—thank *gaaawd*—but you do favor her."

"Who?" Abeo chirped.

39

Abeo spent her days in the house, wondering out at the winter wasteland. The January sun, she quickly discovered, was much like Serafine. Abeo could see it, but it provided little warmth. She learned about America by watching television and reading magazines Serafine left around the house. Books were scarce, and the few that she did stumble across were corny romance novels that bored her to sleep.

Other than that, Abeo migrated through the house, examining the paintings that hung on the walls and ceramic knickknacks perched on the floating wooden shelves. Mostly, though, she listened to the radio while she wrote letters to Taylor and the friends she'd made at Eden.

How are the girls? Have any more of them been reunited with their families? I will send money as soon as I find work. I'm so grateful to you. Serafine said that she will enroll me in school in September. How are Allen, Fannie, and the others doing?

Taylor wrote back:

I miss you, Abeo, and I love you. Some of the girls have

found happy homes. Allen has returned to the States for a while. Fannie has opened a jewelry shop in town and some of the girls work there with her. Don't worry about sending money, your health and happiness are all that I require.

When Ottley dropped in during the day, she scurried to the bathroom and locked herself in until he was gone.

Abeo had taken on the task of cooking dinner, because she missed the food of her homeland and if Serafine had her way, the two would dine on Chinese takeout six nights a week, with pizza on the seventh.

One Saturday afternoon, Serafine and Abeo took the train to Manhattan. Abeo walked with her head tilted toward the sky. The height of the buildings frightened and enthralled her. They strolled down Fifth Avenue, up Park Avenue, and perused the expensive shops on Madison. Serafine bought Abeo a wallet that cost $125.

They ate lunch at a fancy restaurant where the waiter pulled the chair out for Abeo and draped a linen napkin over her lap. Serafine ordered Abeo a glass of champagne. The bubbles tickled her nose and she was giddy before her salad arrived.

Later, on the train ride home, they sat across from a mother and daughter who seemed to ooze with love for one another. As Serafine watched them, something welled up in her and she grabbed hold of Abeo's hand and squeezed. "Did you have fun?"

Abeo was thankful for her touch; there was very little physical contact between them. She squeezed back. "Today was the best day."

40

One night Serafine was awakened by the hollow thump of a plastic pail being set down in the tub. A rush of water followed.

She did not know why it was that Abeo chose to bathe herself in that manner—and she did not ask. Instead she'd said, "You don't have to bathe like a peasant here, Abeo. You can take a shower or even a bath if you want." She'd hoped that the humor in her voice had been clear, but the hurt in Abeo's eyes informed her that it hadn't been, and Serafine never brought it up again. Now, she climbed from her bed, donned her silk robe, and traveled silently down the carpeted hallway toward the study. She didn't knock and was immediately sorry that she hadn't.

Abeo sat naked on the edge of the bed with her scarred back facing the door. Serafine gasped, and when the surprised Abeo swung around, she saw that her daughter's breasts were blemished as well.

Truth be told, she had believed that *trokosi* was akin to indentured servitude and not at all like the slavery that black Americans wailed on and on about. But now she knew that it was indeed the same—the evidence was stamped all across Abeo's body like footprints in sod.

"W-what did they do to you?" Serafine stammered.

"Nothing. It's fine, it's nothing," Abeo mumbled, slipping her gown over her head.

Serafine walked to her, gently pulled the gown from her hands, and used her eyes to scour every inch of her. There were marks everywhere—behind her thighs, on the tops of her feet, on her arms, across her shoulders.

And then Serafine saw the stretch marks across Abeo's belly. They were so faint she'd almost missed them. She looked into her daughter's face. Her voice quaked when she asked, "Do you have a child?"

Abeo lowered her eyes. "I did, but he died."

"What?"

"His name was Pra, and he drowned in the river behind the shrine," she whispered.

Serafine blinked. "What?" she echoed like a parrot. "I-I didn't—why didn't you ever say?"

Abeo shrugged her shoulders. "You never ask about my life in the shrine."

41

The knowing was hard for Serafine; the guilt was even worse. She began to overcompensate for her lies, for her abandonment, buying Abeo more than she needed or wanted—a blouse from Saks, shoes from Bergdorf, a coat from Barneys, scarves from Bloomingdale's. Serafine took her to a high-end salon and had them relax Abeo's tightly coiled hair. She bought her expensive makeup that Abeo would never wear, and perfume that Abeo didn't like but didn't have the heart to tell her.

Serafine thought the gifts would assuage her guilt, but instead it sowed resentment within her. She couldn't pinpoint the time or the place when the bitterness took hold, when Abeo became an intrusion in her life instead of the gift returned to her that she truly was. But it was there, living inside of her, alive and pumping just like her heart.

As a result, Serafine's drinking escalated to the point that Abeo didn't know which Serafine she would be dealing with on any given day. If she was lucky, it was the soupy-eyed, lovey-dovey Serafine. If she was unlucky, it was the Serafine who side-eyed and criticized and then later slunk into her room full of apologies.

The final straw came one weekend when Serafine took Abeo to the mall. She handed her daughter a wad of money, saying, "I'm going to get a mani-pedi. Let's meet back here at two p.m.," and then hurried off to her noon appointment.

Abeo stuffed the money into her pocket and set off in the opposite direction.

She returned to the appointed meeting place ten minutes early. When thirty minutes had lapsed and Serafine still wasn't there, Abeo went looking for her at the nail salon. She wasn't there either.

Two hours later Serafine appeared, visibly intoxicated.

Abeo couldn't hide her annoyance; it shined like a spotlight on her face.

Serafine saw that look and exploded: "Don't you dare look at me that way! You think you're the only one who's had a hard life? I've had a hard fucking life too!"

Abeo cowered beneath Serafine's verbal onslaught.

"I know you blame me for what happened to you, but how was I supposed to know that Wasik would do something like that? Huh?"

Shoppers slowed and stared. Abeo wished herself invisible.

"I brought you here so we could start from scratch, a clean slate, but you don't want that, you want me to feel guilty—and I do. I have for years. Does that make you happy?"

Back at the house, after Serafine had had a nap and two cups of coffee, she came to Abeo swimming with apologies, explanations, and consolations. In the end (as always), Abeo forgave Serafine's waywardness, accepted her good night kiss, and retired to the study.

The next day when Serafine woke, Abeo was gone.

42

Abeo had sat in the dark study, mind whirling. She'd wanted to cry, but she had no tears left, so she balled her fists and used them to club her knees. She wanted to break something and looked around the room for the perfect object to throw. In the end, she removed a picture of Serafine from its gilded frame and tore it to pieces.

She was no longer a child, she was a woman, and with that came strength and power. Taylor had told her and the other girls that they were in control of their destinies—no one else but them. She said that all God wanted was to be loved and for His children to love themselves. She said God had put them on this earth to be happy.

Taylor's words rang in Abeo's head until her anger was replaced with determination. It was time for her to take the reins of her life and set off into the world.

She left the house, Serafine's drunken snores pushing at her back. The streets were empty, save for the stray cats whose eyes turned to gemstones beneath the streetlamps. Following the brightest star in the sky, Abeo headed north toward the train station.

She was certain she saw Ottley's cream BMW cruising toward her. His license plate was unmistakable: *O*

MANI. And she was sure he saw her, because the car slowed and then sped off.

The subway platform was empty. Menacing sounds ricocheted out of the tunnel's dark throat, setting Abeo's imagination on fire.

When the train finally arrived, she stepped hesitantly into the car.

All she had were the clothes on her back, the photo album, and seventy-two dollars tucked into the folds of the Hermès wallet Serafine had given her. She rode the train to the end of the line and back again, then repeated this. The names of the stations meant nothing to her.

A derelict stepped on at 14th Street. He was tall and wide, a matted carpet of gray and black hair covered his head and face. He carried a number of large black plastic bags that clanked loudly with bottles and cans. He took a seat directly across from her and began talking and laughing aloud to himself. Abeo wanted to move to another seat but was too afraid to do so. The man reached into his pocket and pulled out an orange. Abeo watched as he used his filthy fingernails to peel away the bright skin. Her empty stomach grumbled. She caught herself licking her lips as she watched the man sink his jagged teeth into a wedge of the fruit. He swiped at the droplets that settled on his beard, then freed a second wedge and plunged it into his mouth.

When the train pulled into 59th Street, he rose and gathered his belongings. The doors slid open and for the first time he looked directly at Abeo, who was staring fearfully up at him. Before stepping out onto the platform, he reached into his pocket, pulled out another orange, and gingerly placed it down on the seat beside her.

The doors closed, and when the train entered the darkness of the tunnel, Abeo retrieved the orange, peeled it, and quickly gobbled it down.

During the time Abeo sat alone and scared on the train, she had time to ponder her existence in the world, and realized with great awe that she was in fact living a parallel life. A descendant of generations of Ukembans sold into slavery and then, eons later, she, a born American of African descent, had returned to the continent only to suffer the same fate.

The epiphany raised goosebumps on Abeo's arms.

The lights in the subway car blinked, dimmed, and went black. For three very long minutes, the train hurtled through the tunneled passages in darkness as pitch-black as the Ukemban night sky.

Hours later, the car filled with morning commuters. A woman squeezed between Abeo and a young man with a red bow tie. She wriggled her wide hips until Abeo was squashed against the metal arm of the seat.

To distract herself, she opened the photo album on her lap and gazed longingly at the pictures. It took awhile before she realized she was being watched. At first she glanced around, but no one was looking in her direction. Yet when she looked up a second time, her eyes collided with those of a man with graying temples. He smiled and then looked down at the album. His eyes floated back to her face. He seemed to be studying her features. Abeo turned away. Her heart racing, she searched for an escape, but the subway car was crammed to capacity. There was nowhere to run.

"Abeo? Abeo Kata?"

Her name. Her full name was spilling out of this stranger's mouth. Surely she was hallucinating.

She closed the album. How did he know her name? She wished him away, but then he spoke again, this time in Wele: "I'm sorry, you look like someone I used to know."

Abeo's head snapped up. "You are from Ukemby?"

"Yes!" He grinned, relieved. "I knew it! You are all grown up now! Are you living here in New York? Are Ismae and Wasik here too?"

It was Chipo Hama, her old neighbor who Serafine had claimed had a crush on her.

And suddenly, Abeo was weeping.

They exited the train at 34th Street, where Chipo guided her to a graffiti-covered bench.

"I was being nosy," said Chipo, unbuttoning the top of his trench coat. "I was looking down at the pictures in your album, and I thought, *My goodness, those pictures look like they were taken in Ukemby.* But," he laughed and waved his hand, "many African countries look the same. Then I saw Wasik in our younger days," he laughed again, "and I realized that you were little Abeo all grown up."

Abeo sighed and wiped the remaining tears from her eyes.

"So, Abeo, what's the matter?"

The story poured out of her. When she was done, Chipo's face was twisted and limp.

"You will come home with me. My wife will be glad to have you." Then he leaned in and whispered, "She will understand, her sister was *trokosi* too."

Chipo walked to a pay phone next to the turnstiles

and called his wife Femi. They had a brief conversation and then he set the phone down, fished out another coin from his pocket, deposited it into the slot, pressed more numbers, and spoke to a man in his office. With a third coin in his hand, he turned and looked at Abeo. "What is Serafine's number?"

She thought about it for a moment and then retrieved her wallet from her coat pocket, pulled out the card that read, *In Case of Emergency*, and handed it to him.

"Hello?"

"Serafine? Is that Serafine, Ismae's sister?"

There was silence for several seconds. "Uhm. Yes?"

"This is Chipo Hama. You remember me? I remember you. I used to live on Funyan Street, house number 214. This is Serafine, yes?"

There was a long pause. A train pulled noisily into the station, and amid the stampede of commuters, Chipo heard Serafine say: "Yes. What? Why—"

"Good. I am calling to tell you that Abeo is with me."

"Abeo is with you? But how? Uhm, where? I will come and get her."

Chipo covered the mouthpiece with his hand and turned to Abeo. "She wants to come for you."

Her face twisted with alarm. "No, no, please."

Chipo raised his hand and nodded. "Serafine," he spoke into the phone, "Abeo will call you when she is ready. I just wanted you to know that she is in safe hands."

"What? Now you listen to me—"

Chipo hung up.

43

Emerging from the 125th Street train station was like walking into a different world. Harlem's bustling streets were a stark contrast to the quiet, cloistered neighborhood where Serafine lived.

The Harlem air was filled with music, that and the babble of black and brown immigrant tongues from all corners of the world.

They strode past liquor stores, chicken shacks, pizza parlors, and African braiding shops, past merchandise spilling out of storefronts shielded by dozens upon dozens of colorful cotton housedresses flapping in the wind like flags.

On one block, Abeo followed Chipo through a sheath of white smoke rising from an oil drum-turned-barbecue barrel and came out on the other side smelling of jerk pork.

Chipo and his family lived in a gray brick building that towered fifteen stories into the sky. The elevator was a black box with a red door that groaned and bucked like a stubborn old mule. The pair stood silently watching the numbers above the door light up with each floor they ascended.

On the eleventh floor, they exited into a wide,

bright hallway and started across the blue-and-white hexagon-tiled floor. Abeo noted the numbers on the apartment doors and the sounds that pulsed behind them.

Behind the door of 11A a baby cried for its mother. Behind 11C, the melodic beat of steel drums echoed from a stereo. In 11E, two lovers argued about a woman named Dionne.

The hallway was ripe with the aromatic scents of fried fish, stewed meat, and baked bread.

"This one," Chipo said, pointing to a brown door. Below the peephole was a gold decal that read, 11G. Suddenly, the door flung open and there stood his wife Femi. She was short, with soft, wide curves and glittering mocha-colored eyes. Femi rushed past Chipo and threw her meaty arms around Abeo's neck.

"Abeo!" she cried. "Welcome!"

The apartment was small—a box cut up into three rooms with a bathroom the size of a closet. Potted plants covered the windowsills; African violets seemed to be the favorite, the fragile purple petals trembled when Abeo entered the room.

Femi took her by the hand and led her to the couch. "You don't have to say anything. You are welcome here for as long as you like. We are your family now and forever."

Abeo exploded in tears. Femi took her into her arms and rocked her like a baby.

Their two daughters called Abeo *sister* and cleaned out a dresser drawer for the things she would eventually have. The older girl, Kissa, gave Abeo her bed and took the couch. The younger girl, Jelani, said, "You look to be my size. Here is my closet, you can wear whatever you like."

No one minded that she slept with her eyes open and bathed from a bucket because losing Pra the way she did had left her with a severe case of aquaphobia.

"All that will change in time," Femi promised.

"But how can you be sure?" Abeo questioned.

"Because," Femi offered with a smile, "I watched my sister change. It was slow, it was painful, but it happened, and it will happen for you as well."

Abeo nodded. "I see him you know," she breathed.

"Who?"

"Duma. I see Duma."

"Hmm. In your dreams?" Femi asked.

"Yes, there and in the faces of people in magazines, in the faces of strangers on the street, and sometimes I swear I can smell him." Her lips curled into a snarl. "That scent of his—sweat and beer and peanuts." She shuddered. "Then there are those times when I can feel his presence, as if he is standing as close as you are to me right now." Abeo touched Femi's wrist. "The dreams are the worst, though." She moved her hand to her earlobe and tugged it fretfully. "I always die in those dreams."

Femi frowned. "You die?"

"I see him and I take off running. I am running and running as fast as I can, but it is never fast enough—he always catches me and kills me."

The women sat in silence until Femi clapped her hands against her thighs. "Well, Abeo, you must do in your dreams what you are doing in life."

"And what is that?"

"Face your fears head-on. When you dream of Duma

again, you must not run away from him. Run directly to him and then end him."

Abeo set about getting to know her new family and the tightly knit African community. Along with her new sisters, she attended amateur night at the Apollo Theater and laughed at the comedians' jokes even though the punch lines often evaded her. She thought it insensitive the way the audience booed the bad acts, and covered her eyes when the infamous Sand Man, dressed in his hobo tuxedo, came trotting out onto the stage with his hook. The Hama family were Methodists who attended the Mother AME Zion Church on West 137th Street.

Abeo had long ago decided that even after all she'd been through, she still believed in God—but now it was a god of her understanding. That said, she did enjoy the Sunday-morning sermons, the shouting, and the music, and she always left feeling elated.

Eventually, she made a friend, then two. When the phone rang, sometimes it was for her.

Femi smiled, full of happiness for her newest child. "Are you ready to call Serafine yet?" she asked one evening.

A shadow fell over Abeo's face. "Not yet."

"Okay then."

Abeo was able to get a job in a hair shop—a corner space without sinks or hair dryers. Boxes of human and synthetic hair lined the walls, stacked halfway to the ceiling.

"We got all colors," declared Jasmine, the rotund Cameroonian owner. She rustled through one of the boxes and retrieved a dozen packs of hair. "Blond, blue, warm sunset, Kool-Aid red—this one is a very popular color," she laughed, shaking the pack at Abeo.

No appointment necessary. Five chairs, six girls— sometimes twenty fingers worked on one head. All day long, hawkers wandered in and out of the shop:

"I got that new Will Smith movie, ladies! Five dollars, five dollars!"

"Heaven in a bottle, sweetheart, take a sniff of this oil. For you—because you're so beautiful—just three dollars."

"Of course it's real gold!"

"You don't want to buy my music? That's okay. How much do I have to pay to hear your melody?"

To Abeo, Harlem was like Port Masi—like home.

The first week, Abeo came home with $245 and tried to pass the entire roll of money to Femi, who smacked her hand away. "Don't insult me!"

In no time, summer was upon them. The shop door was propped open with an old broom handle. Oscillating fans wafted the heat from one corner to the next.

Abeo suffered through the heat in long-sleeved shirts camouflaging the history on her arms.

But then the day came when a woman walked into the shop with a scar as big as a pancake on the side of her face. She sat down at Abeo's station and talked and laughed as if the disfigurement was as fetching as a beauty mark.

"I want it braided up and into a bun," she explained, pulling the green-and-pink scarf from her head.

When Abeo was done, the woman, Beatrix, grinned at her reflection, applied a coat of gloss to her lips, handed Abeo a twenty-dollar tip, and sauntered out into the heat like a queen with a new crown.

That evening over dinner, Chipo, Femi, and the girls listened intently as Abeo described Beatrix's scarred face and blithe attitude.

"Sister, are you saying she wasn't even wearing foundation?"

"No." Abeo sank her fork into the belly of the deep-fried snapper and yanked away a chunk of flaky white meat. "Just mascara and lip gloss."

"Were the people in the shop not staring at her, sister?"

Abeo nodded. "Some people stared, but she didn't seem to care. I did catch her winking at one person who kept peeping at her."

"Aah, that is a brave woman!"

When Chipo cleared his throat, the women quieted and gazed at him expectantly. "Scars are proof of survival, they shouldn't be hidden—it's a story someone may need to see in order to believe that beyond their pain and suffering, there is healing." Chipo was a man of few words, but when he did speak, he was always profound.

Abeo was inspired. She arrived to work the next day in a short-sleeved shirt. Eyes skirted over the marks on her arms, but not a question was asked until a black American girl plopped down at her station, crossed her shiny legs, and huffed, "You're African, right?"

Abeo nodded.

The girl aimed a lacquered orange fingernail at her right arm. "So those are like tribal scars?"

Abeo thought about it for a moment and finally responded, "Yes, they are."

44

Femi's nephew Dayo Chebe was thirty years old and married to a nursing student named Connie, who had agreed to become his wife for five thousand dollars. He supported himself by driving a taxi, but was planning to go back to school to become a mechanical engineer once his citizenship came through.

Cinnamon-colored, tall, and pudgy, Dayo was hardly ever without a smile. His wry and witty sense of humor kept friends, family, and passengers in stitches. He was well-known and well-loved in and out of his community.

He slept on the couch in the Harlem apartment he shared with his pretend wife. She had a boyfriend named Carl who referred to Dayo as "my brother from another mother" and the two greeted one another with high fives and fist bumps.

A few months after Abeo had moved in with Chipo and his family, Dayo came by for dinner and was so taken with Abeo that he couldn't stop staring at her, which made Abeo so uncomfortable that she excused herself from the table, her plate of *jollof* rice barely touched.

It was a bad habit, this staring. Ukembans tolerated it, but Americans hated it—hated being watched. Even if he was admiring them, they took it as an insult. It wasn't such a problem back in Ukemby. People saw something they liked or didn't like and they gawked until they were satisfied.

Once, when Dayo was still new to America, he was on a downtown bus, sitting across from a group of teenagers who were telling yo' mama jokes and laughing so loudly that the driver threatened to throw them off. A lover of humor, Dayo had watched openly, soaking up every single word.

At one point, a short, chunky boy of fifteen or so narrowed his eyes at Dayo and barked, "Yo, what the fuck you looking at?"

His response was innocent and honest: "You."

After that, Dayo found himself in his first American fistfight.

Yes, he'd stared at her arms, at the faint and fading scars and the raised and golden ones shaped like lightning bolts. But he'd spent so much more time gazing at her pretty face and soft eyes. Truth was, he had a few scars of his own, the remnants of a rambunctious childhood and strict parents. One day, he mused as Abeo hurried away from the table, they might share their war stories and laugh at what had tried to kill them and failed.

After that meal, Dayo began dropping by the apartment more frequently, often arriving unannounced and offering his services. "Do you need me to hang that picture? Replace the shelf bracket?" All the while his eyes were latched onto Abeo, who did not welcome, encourage, or appreciate the attention.

Dayo was perplexed.

"Am I not handsome?" he questioned Femi after Abeo scurried off to her bedroom. He raised his arm and sniffed his pit. "Do I not smell good?" He blew into his palms. "Did Listerine fail me?"

Femi laughed and placed a consoling hand on his shoulder. "She needs time."

"Why?"

"That is for her to explain, not me."

45

For their daughter's eighteenth birthday, Femi and Chipo decided to throw her a big party. The dance hall they chose was an ancient space that had not been properly maintained. The paint was peeling and cracked, the floor tiles were loose or missing, and the bathrooms were dingy, dark, and mildewy. But Femi didn't see any of it—to her it looked like a palace. They rented the space for five hundred dollars, and family and friends devoted two days to decorating the hall.

On the evening of the event, the elder men and women, adorned in their finest frocks and sharpest dashikis, crowded the dance floor alongside teenagers sporting sneakers, jeans, spandex dresses, and incredibly high heels.

Abeo watched from behind the long rectangular tables weighed down with tin pans of food, kept warm with Sterno cans. Foot tapping to the rotation of highlife, R&B, and rap music, she spooned food onto paper plates.

"May I have this dance?"

Dayo had approached from the rear, startling Abeo. She dropped the spoon and it bounced to the floor, sending grains of rice everywhere.

"Oh, I'm sorry," he said, snatching up a roll of paper towels and dropping to his knees. "I didn't mean to scare you." He brushed the rice into a pile and scooped it up.

Dayo excited and terrified Abeo. She so wanted to have a boyfriend; both of her new sisters were giddy in love. To everyone in Abeo's new world, the pairing of men and women was the most natural thing one could do, so why did it seem so unnatural to her?

Femi said the years of abuse—sexual and otherwise—had indeed distorted her perception of men, but that she need not worry, in time she would learn to trust again.

Abeo didn't feel that time alone would solve her problem. She was uncertain she could ever have a man in her life, because Duma wouldn't make room for him. True, Duma no longer had control of her body, but he still colonized her mind and terrorized her dreams.

Abeo knew that only death could truly emancipate her. What she didn't know was which one of them would have to die.

Dayo tossed the soiled paper towels into a nearby garbage can and then turned earnest eyes on her. "Will you dance with me, please?"

Abeo glanced around wildly for help.

When she still hadn't responded to his request, Dayo announced, "I cannot take no for an answer. If you refuse me, I will die." And with that, he collapsed dramatically to the floor.

Abeo laughed in spite of herself. He was silly, that Dayo. Silly and persistent. How could she deny him?

"Get up," she giggled. "The floor is filthy."

They danced a foot apart. Dayo anticipated her every move and his eyes never left hers. After their dance, he escorted her back to the table, fetched her a cup of punch, and lured her into light conversation, which he littered with corny American jokes, causing Abeo to laugh until her sides ached.

"Wow, you carry the sun in your smile!" Dayo exclaimed.

Abeo blushed.

That night, Dayo made Abeo feel like a princess in that broken-down palace of a dance hall.

He began to call her in the evenings and they talked for hours about his job, America, and New York. But when Dayo probed about her life in Ukemby, Abeo quickly changed the subject.

After weeks of asking, and at Femi's insistence, Abeo finally agreed to go to the movies with Dayo. She watched him in the darkness and marveled at the strong outline of his chin, his thick eyelashes, and his white teeth. He was really quite handsome and Abeo felt a strange stirring inside of her. Toward the end of the film, Dayo reached over and touched her hand. Abeo flinched and almost jerked away, but she forced herself to remain still, and after a few minutes found that she liked the feel of him against her flesh.

The next time they were at the movies and Dayo reached for her hand in the darkness, Abeo's fingers curled welcomingly around his.

Once, he bought her a sunflower from a street vendor, and when he presented it to her, Abeo found herself flooded once again with feelings of self-doubt. The distress burned brightly on her face.

"Don't you like it?"

What did he want from her? There were a million women in New York City who he could chose from, so why her? "Of course I do," she stammered.

She shared these haunting insecurities with Femi, who folded her arms around Abeo's shoulders. "The heart wants what it wants. Dayo's wants yours."

"But I'm . . ." she struggled for the right words, "I'm not *clean*."

Femi squeezed her. "Child, you are as clean as if you just arrived here on this earth. The things that were done to you were not of your choosing. God knows that and He does not judge you for it, and if Dayo really cares about you, neither will he."

The first time Dayo tried to kiss her was in the elevator of her apartment building. Abeo reacted like a prize-fighter, dodging his lips and then shoving him so hard, he fell against the wall.

"I'm ruined!" she screamed.

A stunned Dayo slowly righted himself. "I don't know exactly what that means, Abeo, but—"

"It means I can't have sex with you," Abeo stated bluntly.

"What?" Dayo blinked. "I-I never said I wanted to have sex with you, Abeo." He heard himself—the tone, the words—and realized too late that he sounded like an ogre.

He pressed the emergency button on the panel and the elevator came to a shuddering halt. "No," he said, wrapping his arms around his head. "No, that came out wrong. Of course I want to be with you, but only when you're ready."

Abeo had backed herself into a corner. Her statement still hung between them and Dayo had to ask: "Why would you say something like that about yourself?"

Rape was what sex was for Abeo, so how could she possibly make love, or be made love to? She couldn't have this conversation with Dayo, not now, maybe not ever.

He skinned back his teeth, an indication that he was about to say something silly, something that would bring a smile to Abeo's face. He narrowed his eyes suspiciously. "So, uhm, you do have the, uhm, required equipment, don't you?" His attempt to make light of the situation fell flat at Abeo's feet.

"Please press the button that will make the elevator move again," Abeo ordered sternly.

"Aww, Abeo, please don't shut me out. Talk to me. Please." Dayo moved toward her. "I want to understand, Abeo. I care for you so much that I want to know . . . what happened to you in Ukemby?"

Abeo waved her hands. "You do not want to know this, Dayo. Believe me, you do not want to know this."

Dayo pressed further until Abeo finally roared: "I was *trokosi*! I was TROKOSI! Okay? Are you happy now?"

For a second, Dayo's heart, as if attached to a bungee cord, dropped into his stomach and then ricocheted back into his chest before dropping again. He would have never suspected that this was the secret Abeo had been keeping from him. He knew of *trokosi*, familiar with it only because of Femi's sister. Before that, he had always considered *trokosi* something of a myth or a story parents told their young daughters to keep them in line. Now here was Abeo, a cautionary tale come to life.

What was he to do now, turn and run away? He couldn't even if he wanted to—with their heartstrings entangled as they were, he was already bound to her soul; he knew he loved her enough to wait on her body. He could only hope that Abeo felt the same.

He cleared his throat and took a measured step toward her. "Abeo Kata, if *ruined* means perfect then that's what you are to me. I can't change what happened in your past, but I promise you, if you allow me, I will do all that I can to create a future for you that will more than compensate for all that was taken from you. Now, I'm sorry that your journey into my life was such that you had to endure so much suffering. But if that is the road God had you travel in order for our paths to cross, then we have no choice but to accept the purpose it has served and be grateful for it."

46

Six weeks after Dayo took her into his arms, Abeo called Serafine. They met on a warm summer day at a McDonald's near Dayo's apartment. He'd wanted to come along for support, but Abeo declined. "No, I need to do this on my own." But she did agree to call him if things went awry.

Serafine arrived twenty minutes late. Abeo's french fries were cold and the ice in her cup of soda had melted into water.

Serafine rushed into the fast-food restaurant dressed in a pale-blue, sleeveless shift dress. Her gray hair was hidden beneath an auburn pixie wig. It looked to Abeo like she had lost some weight.

Serafine whipped the shades from her face and looked frantically around.

"Auntie Serafine!" Abeo called from across the restaurant.

"Goodness!" Serafine exclaimed, rushing toward her.

At the table, she snatched a napkin from Abeo's tray, rubbed a clean spot on the already-spotless table, and carefully set down her designer purse.

"Why in the world would you choose McDonald's of all places?" Those were her first words. Not: *How have you been? Are you well? I miss you. I'm sorry.*

Serafine's eyes rolled over Abeo's red T-shirt splattered with white hearts. The capped sleeves did nothing to veil the scars on Abeo's arms. In fact, it seemed to Serafine that she had chosen the shirt to purposely place the scars on display. Serafine glanced cautiously around to see if anyone was staring, but nobody was.

"Well, I must say you look very well," Serafine complimented brightly.

Abeo smiled, thanked her, and returned the compliment.

"So," Serafine asked coquettishly, "are you still upset with me?"

"No."

Serafine sighed with relief and rested her clasped hands on the table. "Good, so all is forgiven and we are done with this foolishness. So many months, Abeo. My goodness!"

Abeo stirred the straw in her drink.

"So you can come back home now, right?"

Home? Home was Ukemby. Home was there in Harlem. Serafine's house had never felt like home. Abeo pursed her lips, pulled the straw from the cup, and set it down on the orange tray.

Serafine drummed the table impatiently with her fingernails. "Well?"

Abeo began timidly: "Remember that summer you came to Ukemby and brought me a Big Mac?"

Serafine was puzzled. "What?"

"You brought me a Big Mac. I thought it was the best gift ever."

"Yes, yes, the burger. Didn't we talk about this when you first arrived?"

"We had such a good time. Remember?"

"Yes, of course. But what does this have to do with—"

"That summer I took something from you."

Serafine's back straightened. "You took something? What did you take?"

"A ring with a blue stone. I thought it was so beautiful, so I took it. I thought that if I kept it, it would somehow bring you back to me sooner." Abeo could laugh at the memory now. "And then, after they sent me to the shrine, I thought it was because of the ring. I thought I was being punished for stealing it."

Serafine just stared at her.

"I know now that the ring had nothing to do with it. But it took me a long, long time to realize that . . . I can't come back to live with you," Abeo said, working her hand into the front pocket of her jeans. "I'm happy. I'm working. I'm with people who love me. And that's not to say that *you* don't love me . . . I know you do . . . in your own way." She pulled an object from her pocket and set it down on the table. Serafine looked down at the silver and turquoise stone ring. "I made it myself. I tried to find the stone that was an exact match to the one you had. But that was as impossible as finding identical snowflakes."

Serafine thought it funny that Abeo would use such an analogy. She reached for the ring. "It's beautiful, but I'm not quite sure I understand."

"I don't know that I do either," Abeo responded. "But maybe giving it to you will help us both to start over with each other."

Serafine knew she was a mess. Self-centered and selfish—behavior born out of her feelings of having been discarded by her family. Well, she hadn't wanted to go to America in the first place. And it didn't matter that she would be staying with relatives—they were still strangers. And, really, what was she going to learn in an American school that she couldn't learn in a school right there in Ukemby? Furthermore, Ismae was six years her senior, the firstborn girl, the eldest child—shouldn't she have been the one to be sent abroad?

Serafine had told her parents that she felt as if they were trying to get rid of her because she was smart and outspoken and Ismae was good-looking and compliant, and when it came down to it, Ismae was more likely to attract a husband than she was.

And then, of course, there was the rape.

"R-rape?" Serafine had stammered when the therapist first used the word.

"Yes, rape. You were under the age of consent," the therapist said.

Serafine had never thought of it as rape, because she hadn't said no and he hadn't forced her. "But it's still considered rape?"

"Yes, in the eyes of the law." She handed Serafine the box of Kleenex.

"I didn't believe I could get pregnant the first time I had sex," Serafine sniffed, dabbing at her eyes.

"Uh-huh, a popular and long-standing myth among teenagers," the therapist offered with a smile.

Serafine had nodded, experiencing once again the shame and embarrassment that had flooded her the moment she realized she was with child.

"And when he refused to take responsibility, you felt . . ." The therapist trailed off, leaving Serafine to finish her thought.

"I-I-I felt discarded again." Serafine plucked another tissue from the box and blew her nose.

Eight months after giving birth, Serafine's parents poured salt into her wounds, when she arrived in Ukemby with Abeo and was told—not asked—that the baby would be given to Ismae and her husband to raise as their own.

"And what did you say to that?" asked the therapist.

"I had had a child without the benefit of a husband, and according to the Catholic Church, that made my child illegitimate. In addition, I had brought shame onto my family." Serafine had laughed disgustedly. "What was I to say? My words meant little before I became pregnant and even less after Abeo was born. I was no longer the smart daughter, I was the whore."

The therapist leaned back into the quilted chair and crossed her legs. "Did your parents call you that? Did they actually call you a whore?"

Serafine winced. "Words need not be uttered for one to feel the implications."

And so, Serafine had returned to America with a heart shot full of holes. She finished her education, secured a good job, went looking for love, and for a while fell head over heels for cocaine. She lived with one man for a year, another for six months. Married and divorced and married again.

"The drinking started with my second husband," Serafine said.

"Did you want to have another child?"

Serafine stared the therapist in the eye. "Yes, of course I did."

"So why didn't you?"

"Because after Abeo, I was never able to conceive again."

She wasn't ready to share any of this with Abeo, but she hoped that when she did, it would help the healing of both of their battered and betrayed hearts.

In the time that Abeo had been gone, Serafine had quit drinking and was working on kicking nicotine as well. Her divorce had been finalized and the house was up for sale. She didn't know where she would land, or in what place she would begin the next chapter of her long and complex life. Perhaps, she mused secretly as she marveled at her beautiful daughter, Harlem could become the same happy home for her that Abeo had made it for herself. Perhaps her daughter would agree to be a significant part of that happiness.

Perhaps.

Serafine slipped the ring onto her finger and held her hand up for Abeo to see. "What do you think?"

"It looks good on you."

"It's so beautiful," Serafine murmured, then looked directly at Abeo. "I didn't even kiss you hello!" she piped. Reaching across the table, she grabbed her daughter's hands and brought them to her lips.

Abeo's face lit up with pleasure and surprise. "Oh, Auntie Serafine," she admonished, "people are looking."

"Let them," Serafine laughed. "I missed you very, very much."

And there it was. The words Abeo had longed to hear. They rang out into the air, genuine and clear. "And I you," she said.

"And I'm sorry," Serafine continued after covering

Abeo's hands in more kisses. "I know I've said it before, and although I meant it then, I really truly mean it now. Can you ever forgive me?"

Abeo saw the water swimming in Serafine's eyes and her own eyes began to tear. "Already done."

"I'm trying to be a better person," Serafine said. "I'm trying."

Abeo leaned back in her chair and fingered her hair; her smile turned playful.

"What?" Serafine asked, dabbing the corners of her eyes with her fingers. "What's that look about?"

"There was something else about that summer."

"Uh-hmm?"

"You asked me if I had a boyfriend and I told you that I thought they were yucky," Abeo chuckled. "You said one day that I would like them, that I would love them."

Serafine leaned forward and folded her arms onto the table. "And?"

"And you were right."

AFTER

Abeo brought the screwdriver down into Duma's jugular. Eyes spinning, he stumbled forward, clawing at his neck.

Mohammed shuffled away, screaming for help. Abeo calmly lowered her hand and the screwdriver clanked to the ground.

The blood that pumped from the wound in Duma's throat spiked the humid summer air with the scent of metal. His face was still laced with surprise when he collapsed at her feet.

"Abeo? Abeo!"

She turned around to see a cluster of faces watching her. Faces she was well familiar with: Juba, Nana, Kenya, Aymee, and her son Pra.

She gazed at them in disbelief until one by one they sprouted delicate antennae, colorful wings, and took flight, soaring through the blue sky, over the rainbow, beyond the sun, and out of sight.

"Abeo, wake up. Abeo!"

Her eyes slowly opened; Dayo's concerned face hovered over her. He pressed his warm palm against her wet cheek.

"You were dreaming again."

Abeo swallowed.

"Duma?" he asked, even though he already knew the answer.

"Devil," Abeo whispered.

Dayo drew her into a tight embrace.

"He's dead," she muttered into his chest. "I'm free."

Dayo kissed the top of her head. "That is good. That is very good."

It is 2009, and Abeo is thirty-three years, seven months, and twenty-four days old.

The End

However long the night, the dawn will break.
—African proverb

Gratitude

In 2007, I traveled to Ghana with the National Book Club Conference. On that trip I met and befriended several women, some of whom I'm still in touch with today. But it was a pair of friends, Imelda Price and Linda, who not only made me aware of the practice of ritual servitude in West Africa, but also encouraged me to write about it.

And for that and for them, I am grateful.

As always, I owe a debt of gratitude to my publisher Johnny Temple and his band of brilliant colleagues: Johanna Ingalls, Ibrahim Ahmad, Aaron Petrovich, and Susannah Lawrence.

To my family, friends, and readers, I send my undying love and deepest appreciation.

Light,